The Cat Man

A tragicomic love triangle set in a crazy cat cult

Nick Bruechle

Contact the author:
www.nickbruechle.com
nick@nickbruechle.com
facebook.com/nickbruechlebooks
@nick_bruechle

Editing and proofreading by Hourigan & Co.
http://hourigan.co

ISBN 978-0-6485699-1-6

Set in Adobe Garamond Pro

For my darling wife, Rachel.
And all of our ridiculous cats.

1. Dogs are stupid

Dogs are stupid. They spend their time drooling, dreaming or snarling, and engaged in pointless pastimes like chasing balls or – believe it or not – cats. If you want to be respected for your intelligence, be less like a dog and more like a cat.

Casper

It was one of those late summer days when Perth people stop saying, 'At least it's a dry heat' and just say, 'It's fucking hot.' The eighth day in a row with a maximum on the satanic side of thirty-seven degrees and, right about the time we come into the story, peaking at a fiery forty-one Celsius. The bitumen was blistering and the traffic was seething, and in cars and houses everywhere across the sprawling city, tempers were boiling over.

Rex put his head out of the car window and panted a bit. His coat felt heavy and thick, and his collar seemed intent on choking him. A rivulet of salty sweat ran down his cheek like a tear. Why was he wearing a suit anyway? Was it really necessary? Would she be impressed? Would she even recognise him? He had no idea, but in his fantasy, she swooned the moment she saw him, and he leapt across the gap between them to catch her in a tender but manly swoop while the on-lookers cheered and clapped.

This was perhaps a dream, given that they hadn't communicated much in the year she'd been away, with the few emails that had passed between them early in the piece dropping away to none for the last few months.

He'd written a letter to her once, because he hated 'the email,' as he called it, and he didn't know how else to let her know he was thinking about her. It had been a tough task and it had taken him ages, because he didn't write too often, and he had no idea what to say or how to say it. His beefy carpenter's hands weren't built for holding a pen, and even though he was a smart, well-educated bloke who could hold his own in any pub argument, he didn't articulate well on paper. His thoughts just didn't roll off the pen the way they sounded out in his mind, and his spelling and grammar were, as he had *emitted* to Chloe in his letter, *atroshius*. But he'd put in the effort and had taken care to rewrite it all out again in perfect print, excursions into creative spelling excepted, before sending it.

She'd replied with an eighteen-word email: 'Thanks for the letter, good to hear from you. Very busy and making lots of friends. Love Chloe.' At least there was that last bit. 'Love Chloe.' Could that mean she really did love him? Even he knew that sounded pathetic, but he clung onto it.

The traffic inched along the four lanes of hell he was stuck on, and he tried not to think about their past and the pain of her leaving. That had been a terrible, shocking blow to him. One day she was there, and the next she wasn't, and he didn't understand. Her mother wouldn't say anything, except that Chloe would contact him, and he was confused and lonely and depressed. For the first time in his life he'd become obsessive about checking his emails, and at last the message had come.

'Dear Rexy, greetings from sunny California! I'll be spending the next year interning for a big IT company, working in social media. I'm sorry I didn't tell you I was leaving, but I know you suffer a little bit (okay, a LOT, lol) from separation anxiety, so I thought this would be the best way. Anyway, must fly, people to do and things to meet ha ha. Tata my pet, Chloe.'

Communication since then had been sporadic, and for once his had been the more voluble side of the exchange, intermittent as it was. Chloe didn't initiate electronic conversations often, and she didn't even tell him when, six months in, she left the IT company to go and join some other crowd. The first he knew of it had been when an email bounced back, and further investigation had yielded the information that 'Ms Birman is no longer with the company.'

Still, none of that mattered anymore, because she was coming home. To him, he wanted to believe. After all, they'd been pretty tight when she left. Not together, as in boyfriend and girlfriend or anything, and certainly not ever as lovers. He was more like her friend, her protector, her – well, let's call it what it was – lackey. She relied on him for all sorts of things, and all he needed in return was her gratitude and the opportunity to be with her.

He lived for those moments when they were alone and she was in an affectionate mood. She'd tickle behind his ears, roll her thumb gently across his cheek and unwittingly pull at his whiskers, and ruffle his woolly hair and call him 'pet.' That was about as physical as it ever got between them, but hope sprang eternal in Rex's big hairy chest. One day, he said to himself, she would wake up and realise just how much she loved him, and then they would be together forever.

A gap opened up in the roundabout in front of him, and Rex jammed the pedal to the metal, darting in front of a semi-trailer that was moving a bit faster than he'd first thought. He could see the driver, red-faced and bathed in sweat, yelling and gesticulating at him as he jammed on the brakes, and he laughed and gave the bloke the finger. Fuck him; what was he doing in a big truck like that at peak hour on a stinking hot day anyway?

The last stretch to the airport was much clearer than the rest of Leach Highway, and he was soon pulling into the steel and rubber jungle of the short-term car park. After prowling around like a dentist looking for a cavity for seven solid minutes, he found a parking space and pounced on it, beating an old lady in a battered Gemini by a bee's dick. He wouldn't normally be such a turd, but he was in a hurry, and courtesy is a luxury best reserved for leisurely application.

The afternoon heat beating down onto the ugly expanse of cars and hot, gluey tar was intense and relentless. Great soggy patches of perspiration were spreading from Rex's soaking armpits, and as he crossed the last few metres of pavement to get into the arrivals terminal, the two blooming blobs that were blotting their way across his back, searching for each other, finally met in the middle. A trickle of grimy exudation meandered down his spine, making him even more uncomfortable. His nervousness, which had been growing all day, reached a sudden peak. His vision of a poignant reunion, in which a tearful Chloe fled into his arms – appendages that were now inappropriately sticky, he realised – was evaporating like the damp brine on his forehead. What if she just walked straight past him, the way she'd done so many times at school, even though they were supposed to be friends? ('Secret friends,' was how she'd put it. 'It's much more exciting that way.') Oh, god, what if she'd found someone else while she was away, and had brought him – or her – home? It didn't bear thinking about.

He told himself he shouldn't have come. Wished he wasn't there. He ought to be at cricket practice anyway, and the boys would be pissed off with him. He hoped he wouldn't be dropped for the weekend game, but he doubted he would be; he was the star fielder.

He told himself he'd been a fool for wheedling the flight number and date out of Chloe's mum, who'd only given up the information because she felt sorry for him. At least she had always been on his side. The look on her face when she told him Chloe had left the country had been sympathetic; she had been almost as devastated at her daughter's departure as he was. Telling him the flight details may have been a mother's small way of exacting revenge.

Dammit. He should have gone to practice, then curled up at home and waited for her to come to him. She would come, wouldn't she?

The mob around the opaque glass doors from the customs area reeked of expectation, impatience and BO. People were tapping at their phones, tugging at sweat-stained shorts to stop them from bunching up and sticking to sensitive areas, and looking pissed off. Every time the doors slid open, necks craned and pupils popped, and one or two passengers at most would come out, wide-eyed at the crowd and the heat. Everyone who didn't know those passengers, which of course was almost everyone, tried to look past them to see if their loved ones were coming up behind. It was useless; you can't see into the customs hall, because it has been designed to obscure enquiring vision. The last thing the authorities need is for an outcry caused by some punter in the foyer seeing their husband, wife, son or daughter spread-eagled by begloved Border Force zealots inside. It's not good for public relations.

The door sprang open and there she was, looking as fresh as if she had just stepped out of a milk bath and thrown on that lovely – and, let's face it, quite transparent – white cotton jumpsuit. Her delicate platinum blonde hair fluttered and twirled in the soft breeze caused by the swish of the opening doors, and her dazzling blue eyes didn't so much search the crowd as simply take it all in with imperturbable serenity. Seeing no one that she wanted to, she pushed her trolley towards the exit. Rex's heart melted in much the same way as the rubber soles of his shoes had when he'd crossed the sweltering car park. He moved to intercept Chloe, but he was stuck to the floor.

2. Cats are adorable

Cats are adorable. They win you over with magnetic beauty and hold you in their thrall by sheer force of personality. Their effortless charm, exquisite loveliness and endearing aloofness make cats lovable and loved. Be like a cat.

Casper

As his left foot stuck to the floor, Rex lurched forward with all the grace of a 1985 Ford F100 in which a learner driver has dropped the clutch too abruptly and stalled the engine. He caught Chloe's attention, along with that of almost everyone else in the building, by falling flat on his face. He stood up, his mug blossoming bright red but his cheerful grin fixed, and waved merrily, if redundantly. Chloe's expression didn't change, nor her composure falter, but an astute observer might have said her eyes seemed to have frosted over just a fraction. She didn't smile, but she did wave in a half-hearted, resigned way.

Rex was overjoyed at her reaction, though in an instant he was uncertain. Maybe she was swatting a fly away. Or was it a signal to stop making a spectacle of himself? His gummy shoes made walking difficult as he made his way to Chloe, so he lifted his feet emphatically, like a kitten walking on wet grass. She had recovered that iota of poise that had slipped away when she'd seen him, and she stopped amid the thronging crowd to look stunning and await his lumbering approach. Even the waiting women who instinctively hated her for her inexpressible beauty and unshakeable glamour admired her undeniable freshness despite a long flight.

At last she was but an arm's length away, and he stretched his brawny limbs out towards her, ready for the hug that had been so long in coming. But they met an invisible barrier and hung like useless, floating ham hocks in the air. After a long, inconsolable moment he realised no embrace was forthcoming. He dropped his arms, as limp as his smile had become, to his sides.

'Rexy,' she cooed in a voice that was a blast of chilled air on a hot day. 'You shouldn't have come.'

'Aw, you're just saying that,' he said. 'You know I couldn't stay away.'

'How did you even know I'd be arriving today? Now?'

'Your mum. I managed to wheedle it out of her.'

'I'll have to thank her later,' Chloe said. Her tone did not indicate gratitude. 'But now you're here, you can push this beastly trolley.'

'Of course, I'd love to help.' He stepped closer to her and she backed away, not quite evasively. He took hold of the trolley handle and pushed, but the bloody thing refused to budge.

'Push down on the handle,' she said. 'It has an automatic brake.' And then she smiled with real warmth for the first time, and her eyes sparkled true affection. 'Oh, Rexy, you haven't changed a bit.' Her hand, apparently acting on instinct, flew up to his head to ruffle his hair. Its sweat-soaked dankness made her pull her hand back almost as soon as it made contact, and he guffawed.

'Yeah, it's pretty hot out there,' he said.

'So, is it just you,' said Chloe, scanning the crowd, 'or is Mum coming?'

'Not sure; maybe she decided to leave it to me. After all, we haven't seen each other for a long time. Maybe she thought we should spend some time together?'

'How thoughtful,' said Chloe. 'Again, I'll have to thank her later. But I don't want to impose on you, Rexy, I'll just grab a cab.'

'Hey, it's no drama, I'm happy to do it,' he said. 'It's not as if there's any shortage of space in the ute.'

'No, I suppose not.'

'And we do have a lot of catching up to do. It's so good to see you, it really is. I know we haven't been in touch much lately but I missed you heaps, and I've been looking forward to your coming home. Sorry I'm so shit at the email.'

'Honestly, don't even think about it, sweetie,' she said. At the sound of the endearment, his heart leapt, and he ventured to look straight into her eyes, but they were still probing the crowd with powerful intensity. Without warning, she became fully animated for the first time, and her hand shot up into the air, a flare that burst into a delicate five-pointed star.

'Look, there's Mum,' she said. 'She came!'

'Awesome,' said Rex as his crest commenced falling.

'I'll take that,' said Chloe. She brushed up lightly against Rex as she shoved him out from behind the luggage trolley and started pushing it towards her mum. Stopping a few feet away, she turned and looked at him, standing there with his eyes wide and his lip only just not quivering. She leapt across the space between them and put her arms about him, encircling rather than embracing because he was a trifle wet and tacky, and planted a soft kiss only atoms thick on his cheek. 'Thank you for coming, Rexy,' she said. 'It means a lot.' And then, with a swish and a last flick of her impossibly blonde hair, she was gone, lost in the multitude.

His heart, which had leapt at 'sweetie' and crashed at 'there's Mum,' had leapt again when their bodies met and gone into a complete somersault when she'd kissed him, began to beat a slower, more regular cadence as he made his way back to the scorching car park. He hadn't had to endure such coronary gymnastics for over a year, and his fitness for them had faded. He was sure he'd get back into the habit soon enough. At least, he hoped he would see enough of her to make that happen.

By the time he got home, having replayed the whole scene over several times in his mind, he wasn't so sure. On reflection, she hadn't seemed all that pleased to see him.

3. Cats are diabolical

Cats are infuriating. A cat will never meet your expectations, and will almost always frustrate, annoy and perplex you. It will ignore you when you most need love, and then, just when you begin to accept rejection, will transform into the most charming, loving creature alive. Because that's what keeps life interesting and admirers keen.

Casper

For the next few days, Rex was on a hair trigger. The two teams of chippies that worked for him had never seen him so punchy. He was jumpy, irritable and at times lost in long reveries. Most disturbing, he was – for him – clean and well dressed. His mind wasn't quite on the job, and his heart most certainly wasn't in it, but he wouldn't go home. He prowled around the sites they worked on looking like he was ready to pick a fight, and being unnaturally fastidious about what everyone else was doing without actually picking up a tool himself. Showing a rare attachment to technology, he wouldn't stray more than a metre away from his phone, and spent a lot of time checking that it was on, turned up and connected.

The bloody thing refused to ring, though, and as time went on, he began to suspect Chloe was not going to call. The airport scene played over and over in his mind, and with each retelling became less flattering to his hopes. At the time, he had been tempted to believe that because she hadn't actually recoiled, Chloe had been happy to see him, but in every mental rerun her reaction seemed less convincing.

After three days of pained reflection, a dark time in which it tormented him to refrain from calling Chloe – she frowned on him initiating contact – he resigned himself to the inevitable. She wasn't going to call, because she had moved on. All those years of adoration and service – their 'secret friendship' at school, his endless ferrying her to and from uni, parties, music festivals and other events he was not invited to attend, his instant response to her every whim – meant nothing to her. She had discarded him like a bowl of stale tuna.

A long sigh escaped him as he sat on his couch on the third night of radio silence, toying with his favourite cricket ball. It was over, then. Another year down the gurgler. Twelve months waiting for her to come home to him, and she had come home, but not to him. He sighed again, but then sat up straight.

Well if that was what she wanted, she could have it. He resolved to move on himself, and never look back. He was funny and fit and a devoted friend; he would find someone else to play with. He was even good at making friends when he wanted to – and just look how many mates he had down at the cricket club and the pub.

The pub! He could go down there, knock over a couple of beers and a plate of bangers and mash, and have a yak to the locals. Play some pool. And maybe get talking to some cute girl who wouldn't fuck with his feelings the way Chloe had but would be a good friend, a willing partner and a terrific root. There had been more than a few sly encounters of that nature in the long year she had been away. He jumped up and took a deep breath. Yes! It was time to start a whole new life, and to be the person he was born to be.

He shed his dress work pants and crisply ironed high-vis shirt, and strode into the bathroom to shower. Better be at least a little less stinky for the chicks at the pub. While he was standing under the jets of hot, cleansing water, he replayed the airport scene in his mind one more time, looking for even the slightest hint of encouragement or affection from Chloe. There had been that hug. The aborted hair-tousling. She'd called him sweetie, hadn't she? And let's not forget the kiss. Maybe she did care for him. Perhaps she'd just been tired. Was it possible she really did care but was too shy to show it, and he should take the initiative?

Nah, it was all a show. What could she do? He'd cornered her in the airport, and she'd made the best of an uncomfortable situation. How could he have been so stupid? God, what a waste of time. What a waste of a whole fucking year! Well, he'd show her. He'd … wait, was that the phone? Could it have been the tinkling of the water against the glass screen, or had it been the echo of his ringtone bouncing off the walls from the living room to the bathroom?

The jets stopped, and disregarding the soap bubbles still sliding down his face and chest to create a little foamy mound on his pubes, Rex grabbed his towel and ran wet-footed to the study. He got there just as the phone went ping to signify that someone had left a message.

Tingling with excitement, or at least itching under the drying soap scum, he looked at the screen. One missed call from … Chloe. One message from … Chloe.

Half drying his hands with a quick rub of the towel, he grabbed the phone and hit the button to listen to the voice-mail. The two and a half seconds of preamble, in which the disembodied female voice told him what he already knew – that he had one missed call and one message – seemed to take forever. And then there was her voice, falling like raindrops on the tin roof of an outdoor dunny, soft and musical.

'Hi, Rexy,' she said. 'I meant to call a couple of days ago but it's all so busy and exciting, and I knew you wouldn't mind. But here we are, my dear, in a place where we can get together and restart our delicious friendship. I hope you don't mind, but I've booked us a table at Semicolon, the hip new restaurant bar in Leederville. Eight o'clock tonight. I know it's late notice, but please do come. To my place and pick me up, I mean. See you soon, Rexy, mwah.' As she signed off she laid a moist kiss on the mouthpiece of the phone, delivered to Rex's ear as a slightly metallic-sounding stream of vibrations that charged his mind and made his heart flutter.

Ping, went the phone. Another message from Chloe: 'Don't forget to have a shower, sweetie.' He was already way ahead of her.

He dressed in his best tight jeans and neatest, 'going out' Guns N' Roses t-shirt, and within fifteen minutes of the missed call was on his way to Chloe's place to pick her up. No need to let her know he was coming; they both knew that wild horses wouldn't have kept him away.

4. Cats require unconditional love

Cats are irresistible, and you will fall in love; that's just a given. But the best you can hope for is that the cat allows you to serve them. When that happens, be grateful, be faithful and perform to the best of your ability. One day the cat may even love you back.

Casper

Had she always been so slinky? Smelled so clean and exuded such comfortable sensuality? The answers were "always", "absolutely" and "positively". But when Chloe answered the door, Rex was struck anew by just how captivating she was and how well she wore it. She threw him a great big smile that was as real as it was unexpected, and gave him a lingering peck on the cheek. This time there was no doubt that she was pleased to see him.

Before they even got into the ute, he was head over heels again, and by the time they were around the corner, he was ready to chew his own arm off if she should ask him to. And that was on the strength of about three words spoken. Her greeting had unlocked Rex's confidence and his mouth, so

Chloe kept quiet on the ride to Leederville, resorting to small talk now and then, if only to stem the flow of blather from Rex. She commented on how pretty the lights of the river were as they drove across the freeway. Mentioned that the heat wasn't the same in Perth as in California, but that she preferred the home variety because it wasn't so oppressive. 'It doesn't affect my skin as much,' she said.

'Nothing could affect your skin,' said Rex. 'It's perfect. Like you.' His eyes shone, and if he hadn't been obliged to keep them on the road because he was tailgating the Toyota in front of them, he would have noted Chloe's brief, self-satisfied smile.

Semicolon was – as expected – hip, noisy, crowded and expensive. Chloe fit right in; Rex wished he'd worn another shirt. Preferably silk, open to the navel so he could show off the gold chain he clearly should have had around his neck. That way, he might not have been so different from the rest of the cologne-wearing, Range Rover Evoque-driving men in the crowd. *Wanquers*, he thought, surprising himself with his wit.

Giving the waiter a haughty smile, Chloe ordered two incomprehensibly named and improbably expensive cocktails. Turning to Rex, she gave him a sexy, soul-stoking stare. 'Oh, Rexy, this is so exciting,' she said.

'What?' He was getting excited himself, and hoped it wouldn't show too much.

'I've got something to share with you,' she said. 'Something wonderful.'

'Awesome.'

The hint of a shadow of doubt flickered in her eyes, and he felt he'd let her down already, without knowing why. 'I'm not sure you'll want to share it,' she said.

'Whatever it is, I do,' he said. 'If it will make you happy.'

'Oh, it will, it will. But it will mean some pretty major changes in your life, and I'm not sure you're ready.'

Holy shit – was she going to ask him to marry her? The answer was yes. Did she want to move in with him? He'd redecorate. Whatever it was, he was committed before she opened her mouth.

'I've joined a group,' she said.

A group? That was disappointing. He was already planning the jarrah wardrobe he would build for her in their room, and designing a new kitchen. How the hell was he going to fit a group in there?

'Oh.' His voice had flatlined along with his heart. 'What sort of group?'

'It's kind of a religion,' she said. 'We call it a church for tax reasons, but Casper says it's really more of a way of life. There aren't any religious ceremonies or anything.'

'Casper?' He repeated the only word that had stuck.

'He's the founder of our church. It's called Felinism.'

'Felinism?' He was starting to feel like an echo chamber.

'It's a wonderful philosophy, and so simple it's just hilarious. But once you start to get it, it will make your life so much easier and more fun, and then later it gets really intense and mind-blowing. It's like nothing you've ever dreamed of before. Do you want me to tell you about it?'

'Sure.'

'Okay.' She took a deep draught of her cocktail, and he was mesmerised by how slender and elegant her fingers were, how the dazzling ice-blue light seemed to come from behind her eyes, and how the muscles in her neck worked so delicately to swallow the creamy liquid he would be paying over twenty dollars for.

'As you know, I was working for an IT firm in Silicon Valley. It was great, but it was a bit boring, really, just working on software and productivity apps, which are a huge yawn. After a few months, I had some holidays, so me and my friend hired a car and drove all the way down the coast to Baja California, which is just amazing and everyone should do it. Omigod, Tijuana is such a blast! But that's a whole other story, with lots of tequila and cerveza and sun and sand and surfers and starry nights...'

She stopped because she could see Rex had started to wear his sad face when she'd mentioned surfers. She took another long sip. 'So, on the way back, we stopped in San Diego and we went into this darling little cafe where they have cats. It was gorgeous, and so relaxing. I've always loved cats, and this was just divine – people were watching cat videos and sharing cat photos, and you could even have a sweet little pussycat on your lap while you had a coffee. It was heavenly. Well, who should be there but the guy who runs the whole thing, Casper White. He's an Australian, from Sydney, but he lives in California because that's where all the clever people go. He has this idea that people should be more like cats.'

'Cats?' Yep, he'd become a permanent echo chamber.

'Yes, cats. There's much more to it, but that's the essence of Felinism: to help people become more like cats.'

'Um, why?'

'Because cats are the most surprising and intelligent creatures on earth. They're cool, they're self-assured and confident, they don't need anyone or anything, and if they give their love, they do it freely and genuinely. Casper says that if we all behaved more like cats, the world would be a better place. He's set up a bunch of Cat Life Centres across the States, and people go there to be with cats and to learn from them. It's beautiful.'

Rex snorted some milky gunk out of his nose. 'Sorry,' he said. 'It sounds kind of stupid.'

A light flared in Chloe's eyes, like the flash of pure energy that radiates out from a nuclear explosion before the shock-wave hits. But the convulsion didn't follow. She pursed her lips and looked miffed, but there was something about her manner that said she'd been expecting a reaction like that. Rex was sorry he'd set off this chain reaction, and wished he could take his flippant retort back.

'Don't take this the wrong way,' said Chloe, leaning forward and penetrating his skull with her beamy eyes, 'but you're a bit of a dog, Rex.'

How could he take that the wrong way? Was there a right way? He wasn't far from bristling, and when he tried to smile it looked like he was baring his teeth. 'What do you mean?'

Chloe didn't back away. 'Casper says that some people, like me, are naturally catlike, but some people, like you, are more like dogs.'

'Does he know me, this Casper bloke?'

'No, he doesn't mean you in particular, silly, he means in general. Some people are like sheep, or rats, or birds and so on. Remember Mrs Campine, the French teacher? The one with the sharp nose and the angry strut, who ran around pecking at everyone? Well, she was a chicken, personality-wise. And the biology teacher, Aspinall. He was a snake if ever I've seen one. So people can be any animals really, but a lot are cats or dogs. And there's nothing wrong with being a dog – it means you're loyal, loving, accepting and full of energy, among other things – but if you really want to get on in life, you should try and be more like a cat.'

'I see.' He didn't see at all, but he didn't want to go back to that nuclear detonation phase either. Next time the shockwave might follow and turn him to dust. He had to admit to himself, as well, that Chloe had always been quite catlike. She had that wonderful grace and dignity, that unruffled steadiness and serenity. It was part of what attracted him. He wondered if he was drawn to her because she was a cat and he was a dog, and whether he was destined to spend his life chasing but never catching her. It was disconcerting to think of it that way.

'So, I spent like five minutes with Casper and I knew that he was like no one else I've ever met before and that I needed to find out more about his religion. Fortunately, he took to me as well, and he was very keen on having me join the church. So I quit my job there and then, just phoned my resignation in and joined. I've been working for Casper for months now, and I'm fully invested in Felinism as a Level Three member, so I know the whole, beautiful truth. You can't know that yet; you can only be initiated once you commit to becoming more like a cat – joining at Level One.'

'So how do I do that?'

Chloe reached out and stroked his hand with the lightest feather touch, sending a thrill through his entire body. 'Join me, and join the church,' she said. 'Help me set up the first Perth Cat Life Centre, learn about Felinism and be more like a cat. I promise you it will change your life.'

Suddenly, being a dog didn't seem such a bad thing to be, and Rex wasn't sure he wanted to be too much more like a cat. As far as he was concerned, they were self-centred narcissists who lay around all day, and at night went out and murdered innocent creatures for the sport of it. On the other hand, being more like a cat – or at least pretending to want to be – was his big chance at spending more time with Chloe. And he didn't want to blow that. Besides, he told himself, he was open-minded: maybe he would learn something. Somewhere in the back of his big doggy brain, something chuckled. He'd have a crack at becoming more like fucking Godzilla if it meant spending more quality time with Chloe.

'So, tell me more about this thing, this Felony...'

'Felinism,' she corrected. 'Casper says, and I agree with him, that cats are the smartest creatures on earth. He says they're superior even to humans, and because they are so much better than us, it's only natural for us to want to emulate them. Be more like a cat, and you'll be better than the other humans around you.'

'What makes this Casper think cats are better than people?'

'Think about it, Rexy. Cats spend their lives doing whatever they want, and they have this amazing ability to get humans to do their bidding. If a cat wants you to open the door, you always end up opening the door. If a cat wants to be fed, it will make you feed it. And if it wants to sit on your lap and be patted, it will just get up there and you'll end up patting it. Casper says it's because humans are really cats' servants, and we should recognise that. Our Cat Life Centres are all about helping people realise how much smarter and more in charge cats are, and giving them an appreciation of cats' lives. We show them the fun side of cats through cat videos and memes and pictures, and when newcomers start to understand just how important cats are, we sign them up to the group.'

'Does it work?' Rex was still struggling with the notion that cats were smarter than him.

'There are nine Cat Life Centres in California alone, with another four in New York, three in Florida and twenty-five across the other US states,' Chloe said. You could hear the pride in her voice. 'Not only that, Casper has some famous actors on-board, and some of them are now Level Three Felinists.'

'What's Level Three?'

'Casper's theory has a scientific basis.' She smiled knowingly. 'But until you've proven that you're willing to commit to the group, and sworn the oath of secrecy, you can't learn it all. But I can tell you this: it's incredibly exciting and it makes a lot of sense, and it will make you a better person.'

'Really?' In spite of himself, Rex was intrigued. He'd never been one for trying to better himself – he knew he had a few flaws, but overall he reckoned he was fine, so he'd never seen the point. Except where Chloe was concerned, of course – in that one area he was kind of shit. But he didn't know of any self-improvement course that would fix that.

'If you help me out, Rexy, I'll give you the background and induct you to Level One and maybe Level Two Felinism. It's easy to learn the basics. I won't do as good a job as Casper, of course. He's so smart, and such a cat. So confident and smooth, and people are just drawn to him the way they are to cats. You should see the way he interacts with all those famous people, like he was just born to be with them. To rule them, even.'

Rex figured he'd have to go along with the whole trip, not necessarily to become a cat, but to stay close to Chloe and find out more about this Casper cat.

'So, what do you want from me?'

A broad, triumphant smile appeared on Chloe's face, and her eyes smouldered with satisfaction. Stroking Rex's arm with one hand, she raised the other at a passing waiter and barked out an order for two more of those revolting cocktails. Rex yearned for a beer, but he wondered if they even sold beer in a place like Semicolon; if they did it was probably from some Swiss monkery, and thirty dollars a stubby.

'Casper has asked me to set up Australia's first Cat Life Centre right here in Perth,' said Chloe with a glow. 'Can you imagine that? It's a huge job. I have to get a property in a hot suburb like Peppy Grove or Subiaco, or here in Leederville – although these people look kind of doggy to me, maybe Subi would be better – and fit it out as a Cat Life Centre. That means signage, free internet terminals everywhere dedicated to cat-related sites, cafe stuff like coffee machines and fridges, and of course plenty of nooks, towers, playthings and bedding for the cats.'

'Cats?' Rex was back to being an echo chamber.

'Of course, silly,' she said, swatting his hand. 'You can't have a Cat Life Centre without cats. I need, I dunno, at least ten, maybe more of them. It's going to be wild!'

Rex pictured a chaos of fur, fights, spray and cat shit ejected at random all over the place, and had to agree – it would be wild indeed.

'So I need you to do the fit-out, Rexy,' Chloe said. It was more of a subtle command than a request, and Rex knew he was committed whether he liked it or not. Still, his company had the capacity because work was a bit light on right then, and he could probably gouge this Casper bloke for a dollar or three, so why not? He nodded, and Chloe licked her lips. 'I knew you'd do it,' she said. 'You're such a good boy.'

5. Cats are promiscuous

Cats will withhold their affections from you despite your avid attention to their every need, and then confound you by showering the most delirious love and intimate caresses on the next stranger to happen by. This apparently cruel and wanton behaviour will only sharpen your desire for their regard and stiffen your resolve to be worthy of their appreciation.

Casper

'When I was in California, I ran the social media side of Felinism,' said Chloe between sips of yet another cocktail. 'I had a team of people who find and propagate content regarding cats across every social media platform there is – the big ones like Facebook and Twitter and Snapchat and Pinterest, Reddit, YouTube, Instagram, of course, plus a whole hive of smaller ones. There are so many of them, it's actually a little bit scary.'

Rex had no idea what she was talking about. What the hell was content, and how the fuck would you propagate it? He nodded, and fingered the stem of his cocktail glass, looking glum. He was glad the drink was so revolting, because this was his third and he probably shouldn't have any more if he was going to drive them home without collecting a lamp post on the way.

'It's wonderful,' Chloe glowed. 'There are so many millions of cat lovers out there that finding cute and funny and simply adorable pictures and videos and memes and stories about cats is easy, and every single one of them just makes me love cats more. Casper says I'm a natural cat anyway, so I have a knack of choosing content that makes cats more appealing and lovable. He says people are drawn to me the way they're drawn to cats, because I have the same ability that cats have of getting people to just do things for them.'

Given that he'd just signed up to build a cat centre and was racking up a bill that would keep a cat in fillet steak for a fortnight, Rex couldn't disagree with that assessment of Chloe's persuasive capabilities. But the repeated mention of this Casper punter was getting on his nerves, and between that and the impenetrable technological bent of her job explanation, he was getting restless. He wanted to scratch his nuts but figured that might turn her off. He licked his lips.

'So, tell me more about this Casper dude,' he said. *God, I am a sucker for punishment.*

'Oh, he's just wonderful,' said Chloe. Her pupils widened, and Rex was pretty sure that beneath her sheer white blouse her nipples hardened. He wanted to tear Casper's throat out. 'He's so smart and so feline, so in touch with the way cats are and so connected to what makes people tick. He can get anyone to do anything just by thinking about it, almost. And when he talks about cats, you just know that his link with them is genuine. It's like they talk to him and he can talk back. You should see him with his cats. He has about twenty of them and they just adore him. He's developed this whole complex philosophy and discovered the true history of the relationship between cats and humans, and turned it into this amazing group that makes people happy and contented and independent, just because by being with him and learning from him they become more like cats.'

It sounded to Rex like this Casper joker was particularly adept at snowing people, but he kept that thought to himself. He couldn't stay wholly silent, though, because a suspicion was gnawing at him that he couldn't dismiss. He didn't want to be snappy, but he couldn't help himself. 'So, have you slept with this Casper cat?'

Still in a dreamy state over mister wonderful Cat Man, Chloe didn't even blink. 'Of course,' she said. 'He's a tomcat, and when female cats are on heat, they mate with the alpha tom. And there is no question that he is the alpha tom.' She seemed then to wake up of a sudden and realise what she was confessing – or rather, to whom. She had the good sense to blush and take a demure sip of her drink. 'Sorry to be so blunt, Rexy,' she said. 'But you did ask.'

Rex wished he hadn't asked. In fact, he wished he was at home chewing his blanket. He couldn't count the nights he'd lain at home, wishing he could get some tiny sign of affection out of Chloe. Just a kiss! Perhaps a quick feel in the ute. But all his life there had been nothing more than an occasional morsel – a peck here or a hair-ruffle there, just enough to keep him interested, and always at that critical juncture when he was thinking it was all too hard. And she'd admitted to fucking this Casper bastard so readily! Jesus, he must really be something.

Chloe, meanwhile, had assumed an attitude of regal reserve. Her look said, 'You asked the question, so you have to put up with the answer.' Modest, apologetic Chloe was gone. But he knew that no matter how poorly he took her frank admission, or how sceptical he might be about this whole cat caper, he couldn't wriggle out of it now. And by god, if being more like a cat was what it would take to win her, then that was what he would do. He would prove to mister alpha tom just who the top cat really was, even if he had to claw that fucker's eyes out to do it. Besides, he knew she was prepared to walk away from him if he didn't suck it up and move on. It cost him dearly, but he grinned and said, 'Well, I'd better learn how to be an alpha tom, then.'

For the rest of the night, Chloe slurped cocktails without getting the slightest bit drunk, and talked to Rex about how to be more like a cat. 'Cats don't need validation,' she said, in what sounded a bit like an admonition. 'They aren't needy, and they don't require anyone else's consent. They just do what they do. That's why you ought to be more like a cat, Rexy. Because it's a bit of a doggy thing to be seeking approval all the time.' And so on. By the end of the night, Rex wondered if he ever could be a cat man, because according to Chloe, he was so deeply doggy he practically had fur.

He dropped her at home sometime after midnight, and for his trouble received a peck on the cheek and a scratch under the chin. She also extracted confirmation that he would design and construct the Cat Life Centre, preferably without too many of his grubby carpenter friends involved. 'Just send them off to do all those other boring jobs, darling, and give me your undivided attention. Don't worry, Casper will pay you, and well,' she said. 'He's given me access to a bank account with a huge pile of money in it, and I can spend whatever I need to get the centre happening. I just need a few days to start getting it all together – finding a property, getting cats organised and maybe recruiting a couple of cat hostesses and cafe staff. I'll call you in a week or so.'

6. Dogs are indefatigable

They may be big, dumb animals, but dogs are hard-working, reliable and almost inexhaustible. They will run all day if you ask them to, and in fact this is the best outcome, because when it's over they will sleep like the babies they are, so you can get on with being like a cat.

Casper

Three long, hard, increasingly heartbroken weeks later, Chloe called. By that time, Rex had convinced himself that his reaction to her slutty behaviour with Casper the stud had turned her off him, and that he'd missed his chance for good. He moped around, bit the heads off his staff on-site, and barked long strings of short words at every driver who crossed him – and on Perth roads, that's a lot of drivers. He came home irritable, ate near-raw steak by tearing it to pieces, and went to bed early and pissed off. He woke up the same way and repeated the whole process with a scowl.

And then she called. What a change that made in his demeanour. In a flash, he was the old happy, helpful, harmless

Rex that everyone loved but not too many respected because he was so much of a pushover. But he didn't care: he was talking to Chloe.

'I've got a property in Rokeby Road,' she said. 'Word is that Subi is falling apart because greedy landlords are bleeding the shop owners dry, so there's plenty of vacant space. Of course, you'll need only the best of everything, but Casper will pay. He's got a lot of rich, generous members now, so it's not a problem. Can we start next week?'

Rex had promised a customer he'd build her new kitchen the next week, but he was sure she wouldn't mind waiting another fortnight or so. She'd been doing a complete renovation on her house, so she was used to dealing with tradies and she must have known by then that they could be a little capricious with their time. He wondered if he should call and tell her, or just not show up. Probably best not to call; it would only piss her off. She'd figure it out sooner or later.

'Sure,' he said to Chloe. 'Next week sounds great. Have you got a floor plan?'

'I've got a few chook scratchings,' she said. 'Is that enough?'

'I'm sure we can work something out.' Working things out entailed Rex producing a beautifully rendered design and some proper working drawings from Chloe's sketches. The secret to his success as a carpenter was that he was something of a design genius, but he didn't charge design fees because he thought it was all part of the job. Although he charged top dollar for his carpentry, the punters who commissioned him soon worked out that they were onto a good thing, and they spread his reputation for him. This was another reason the kitchen lady would be content to wait.

After sending a copy to Casper and receiving his approval, Chloe gushed over the design and gave Rex a proper hug for doing such a terrific job, which almost made all that hard work worth it. And just like that, they were off on an adventure together. Well, sort of. Not quite.

He measured the gutted former kebab shop in Subiaco by himself, and with his offsider Tommy helping to move all the heavy items in, got started building the thing. Chloe spent her days out 'getting things done.' This included buying computers and monitors; furniture that looked way too expensive for cats to be crawling all over, let alone clawing and tearing up out of sheer ennui; brand-new coffee machines; sandwich presses and other cafe kitchen essentials; fridges and washers; original pieces of artwork, and much more. She also recruited a horde of people for the new centre – baristas and cooks, an IT fellow named Dexter, a social media assistant and a marketing coordinator to work with her, waiters, cleaners, cat wranglers, and an office slash accounts manager.

Every afternoon she would breeze in and prowl around, liking this and disliking that, giving Rex orders as to what must be changed and what must be done, feeling all the soft furnishings and admiring her reflection in the hard surfaces – and then she would breeze out again. In the meantime, Rex worked like a dog, racked up an enormous bill at Bunnings, and made everything perfect, just the way Chloe wanted it. At night, he went home pooped, but pumped at the fact that he and Chloe were 'working together,' and after dinner he curled up on the couch by the phone in case she should call. Most nights she did, just to check on the day's progress and provide effusive encouragement, which gave him the energy to attack the next day's toil.

In a couple of whirlwind weeks, it was all done. The place was a shiny palace, a haven of comfort and indulgence for cats and people alike, with a welcome atmosphere and a bright neon sign, and more cats than Rex had ever seen in one place. Chloe had employed three people – Sophie and Jasper, the cat carers and groomers, and Cheyenne, a registered vet nurse, to look after the animals, and in no time at all they seemed perfectly at home together. Of course there had been one or two misfits who insisted on staking unreasonable territorial claims or were just plain cantankerous, but these had been returned to the shelters they came from.

'Cats are just like humans,' said Cheyenne. 'Some get a little bit cranky in their old age, some like their personal space more than others and some are just arseholes.'

Rex figured Cheyenne was definitely in the right place. In fact, all the new staff seemed well suited to their new jobs. They were all, according to his newly developed 'cat radar,' very catlike people – all silky and cool, vain and aloof when they wanted to be but disarmingly charming when they wished. And every one of them was alluringly attractive. Rex felt like an outsized oaf around them, and none of them sought to put him at ease about it. They just accepted that was the way things were.

'See how feline they are?' Chloe said to him. 'How effortlessly things come to them and how people are drawn to them? They're all natural Felinists and they didn't even know it. But I've been trained, and I knew it the moment I saw them all. Watch these people, Rexy, and try to be more like them.'

Rex grunted. He thought the men were all gay and the women were all bitches, to be honest, and he resented the way they acted like he wasn't there most of the time. *I may be a dog*, he thought to himself, *but I didn't see any of these motherfuckers building a fucking cafe.*

7. Cats are fascinating

Awake or asleep, at play or in a meditative pose, eating or demanding attention, cats are endless sources of fascination, beauty and charm. Being beguiling and enchanting comes naturally to a cat – and when it comes naturally to you, you will be more like a cat.

Casper

The Cat Life Centre was everything Chloe hoped it would be and more. Rex had worked his ring off making it happen, and she was being honest when she said she thought it was the best Cat Life Centre in the world. She had been generous in her praise of Rex's design and construction skills, and he'd felt the bond between them growing. The only downer came when she said that of course the real credit had to go to Casper. He was such a genius. He'd worked the whole process out to perfection, and from the very first day the first Cat Life Centre was open, it had worked. How could it not? It was pure, inspired brilliance.

Rex had said to himself, half in contempt and half in despair at Chloe's preoccupation with this mysterious character, that Casper's model wasn't unique. Others had enjoyed enormous success using similar formulas, and he had taken their good work and made it his own, adding his characteristic panache.

'The first thing,' Casper had said to Chloe back in San Diego, 'is to get the punters in.' He may have been in the United States for a long time, but he was still very much an Aussie boy – and that meant using expressions that Yanks found perplexing, disappearing to watch interminable cricket matches at inopportune times, and drinking his own body weight in beer at least once a week. She loved that about him – he was such a cat that he did everything he wanted to and nothing that he did not.

'Now, the trick is not to let the cat out of the bag, so to speak,' he'd continued with a wink. 'No one is going to come into our Cat Life Centres if we tell 'em we're going to sign 'em up for our religion. So we just give 'em what we know they want – and that's cats.'

Ever since the internet had come along to enrich everyone's lives with inescapable connectivity, total loss of privacy and unceasing torrents of useless infotainment, one species of animal had dominated its ever-broadening bandwidth more than any other, and that was cats. People just could not get enough videos, images, memes, tweets, tropes, ads and stories featuring cats of all shapes, sizes, temperaments and dispositions. Over 500 million cat videos alone zipped along the fibre optic cables and whizzed across the wi-fi airwaves of the world. There were almost half a billion photographs of cats tagged #cats or #catstagram on Instagram, and a cat labelled as 'the world's grumpiest cat' because of his odd physiognomy had millions and millions of followers across a raft of social media platforms, and had netted his owners a tidy fortune – until he died, which must have been a massive blow to their bank manager.

Everywhere you looked, there were cats being brave, silly, loving, cold, cuddly, cute, sweet, vicious, nasty, loving, wet, scared, scathing, curious, charismatic, brutal, imperturbable, cunning, mysterious and unforgettable. The entire globe was awash with cat love – as it still is today – and Casper knew that these photogenically playful, predatory, provocative, indolent, indomitable, irresistible balls of fluff and fur would be his ticket to fame, followers and filthy lucre.

The very first Cat Life Centre had set the scene for all the others that were to follow. They may have looked like cafes that were stocked with cats along with coffee and cakes, but they were so much more. You didn't have to buy a coffee or sit down for a meal gratuitously laced with several grades of cat hair – you could just drop in and watch a few cat videos, look at cat pictures on any of a hundred social media apps, play with, talk to, pet and be scratched by the in-house cats, take their photos and post them on your own sites, and even have a free chat with a veterinarian nurse about your own pussy's problems. There were no strings attached – you could do any or all of these things unmolested and unfettered, any time. But those so inclined could also sign up to get free updates including funny and engaging cat videos and photographs on-line, invitations to special cat-based events and parties, loyalty and cat-owner discounts, and so much more.

All you had to do to gain entry into this vast and growing society was to answer a few probing questions about your life, your mind, your hopes and dreams, and your cat. But even cat ownership was optional – the only thing any prospective member really needed was an inclination to credulity.

Hundreds of thousands of people had given Casper the keys to their inner lives so they could be a part of Cat Life, and a lot of them were watching online on April first when the Subiaco Cat Life opened to great fanfare – which frightened some of the cats inside. The cats' terror made all those on-site and web-watching chuckle and titter, such was their affinity for felines.

The one thing everyone in the cafe had in common with the army of feline fanatics watching online was that they had all answered yes to the pivotal question, 'Would you like to be more like a cat?' That was the key to becoming a Felinist and beginning to be initiated into the mysteries of Casper's religion. For the small price of just ten dollars a month, payable annually, Felinists received regular missives from Casper, access to videos and written works in which he personally instructed them in their approved level of Felinist theory and action, and entry into a growing global community of like-minded people who wished to learn how to be as independent and individualistic as the cats they venerated. For many, there was a great deal of pride in knowing that just by saying it was so, they were more like cats than their neighbours, workmates and friends.

Chloe had seen the spectacular growth of Felinism first hand in her time working for the church. Indeed, with her skills in social media and her actual literacy – a perceptible advantage over so many others in the organisation – she had played an important role in that growth.

She had risen in the ranks as a result of her undeniable competence, her extreme attractiveness and her welcoming of Casper's physical attentions. A fellow Australian who was having such an excellent impact on his business and combined that with the energy and stamina to regularly act as molly to his tom was bound to win Casper's favour, and she was one of several similarly talented and disposed Aussies on the team. He had been delighted to personally initiate her into the secrets of the religion at the very highest levels.

So here she was, presiding over Australia's first Cat Life Centre, in daily contact with the feline guru himself, and loving life. The only thorn in her paw, as it were, was Rex. He was all over her like a cheap suit, spending an inordinate amount of his free time in the Cat Life Centre. In one respect, this was a good thing. He had clearly taken her injunction to be more like a cat – in his case just less like a dog would be an improvement – seriously. And there were many times when he was handy to have around to do some heavy lifting, or even just to talk to. It was just that there were also times when she had to find somewhere else she needed to be, because his conversation, his unyielding attachment to her, or his personal fragrance, had become burdensome.

8. Cats are persuasive

Cats are persuasive. They have a seductive aura from which no one is safe, and their logic, though icy cold, can generate white heat within you. Unless you're made of stone, or are as dumb as a dog, you'll do what the cat wants. Be like a cat.

Casper

It was early Monday morning, and the Cat Life Centre staff were standing around with their coffees and teas, chatting about their weekends or petting the residents. Chloe called them to attention, which took a few minutes because they had all internalised the idea that cats don't follow orders unless coerced, so she could give them their daily pep talk. Given that as Cat Life Centre employees they must undertake some tasks normally considered distasteful to cats, like being pleasant to customers and evangelising their religion, the staff needed regular indoctrination sessions like these to hone some of their Felinist behaviours.

Dressed in one of her trademark flowing jumpsuits, with her hair left sinuously free and her expression set to satisfaction, Chloe was as catlike as it is possible for a human to be, and her staff loved her for it and wished dearly to emulate her. Each of them had applied for a job at the Cat Life Centre because they felt they had a lifelong affinity with and affection for cats, and when Chloe had revealed to them that it was because they were born Felinists, it was an epiphany. Suddenly their tendencies towards indifference, indolence, fickleness and cunning, and the disdain for others they felt were beneath them, all made sense. It made them blossom and gave them an inner peace that most of them had never known. Still, they had been told repeatedly that to become true Felinists they must study Casper's teachings and help customers to realise that Felinism was the way of life they should be embracing. The sliding scale of bonuses attached to signing up new paying Felinist members was instrumental in motivating them to overcome their natural aversion to servile behaviour and stoop to talking to ordinary people in cordial tones.

'This is so exciting,' said Chloe. 'Thank you all for coming so early on a Monday morning. I hope you're all as thrilled as I am. We are here to create something wonderful for the people of Perth – something many people around the world have already adopted as their faith. Yes, I use the word faith, because Felinism is a religion. You'll see that when you are initiated into the next level, as you all will be. When you signed your employment contracts, you all agreed to regular donations to the Church of Felinism, and those donations entitle you to graduate to Level Two. But for now, we'll start with Level One.

'You all have your handbooks and your instructional videos from Casper, so I don't need to go into too much detail here. But in Level One, the novice is encouraged to spend a lot of time with cats, to watch how they behave and to learn from them. In this, you'll be aided by Casper's wonderful words and ideas, and because you're all new to this, I expect you to help each other. The thing is, at this level you need to be conscious of being more catlike at all times. Think about everything you do and ask yourself, would a cat do it this way?

'It can be tough at this level, because as you'll discover, sometimes being more like a cat can seem rude or dismissive to other people, and at times you'll need to be quite pitiless. But once catlike behaviour is instinctive, hurting other people's feelings won't seem so bad, and you'll see just how much more others respect and admire you. If you have the self-assurance and poise to walk away from someone who is struggling to accept your feline inclinations and Felinist beliefs – to cut them off and never give them another thought – you'll see that they'll soon come around, and they will love you all the more for your passion and commitment. If for some reason they are obstinate and insist that you choose them over your beliefs, you're better off without them.

'Your job here puts you in a prime position to immerse yourself in Felinism and to fast-track your development as cats. It will also expose you to lots of different kinds of people, and you'll be able to see for yourselves the positive changes in those who commit their minds and their lives to our faith. Your job may be waiting tables, making coffees or helping customers engage with our cats, but your vocation is to help us create a world full of cats. Imagine just how wonderful it will be when we're all cats! Every one of us will have inner serenity, be able to switch off and sleep soundly any time and anywhere, and we will all know where we stand with one another. Sure, there will be catfights, because every one of us will stand our ground whenever there is conflict, or if the whim to fight just takes us. But even these instances can be instructive, empowering and fun. And the pleasure you'll take in decimating enemies who are less catlike than you is truly delicious.

'Now, we're about to open the doors for another week of cat-loving fun, engaging with cat-fanciers and recruiting new devotees to Casper's wonderful religion. I urge you all – be catlike, have a terrific time and bring in more converts. On your own time, curl up in a corner with the books and DVDs provided, and spend as much time as you can online promoting Felinism and cats in general. And above all, live by our unwritten rule: share, share, share everything on your social media channels.'

'Why is that an unwritten rule?' asked Bert, one of the baristas.

Chloe smiled a cold, toothy smile that edged towards being a grimace. 'Well, Bert,' she said in an icy tone, 'it's not really very catlike behaviour to share, is it? It's not something we cats like to do, for any number of reasons, the least of which is that sharing implies a certain camaraderie with others who are not worthy of being considered our equals. But it is catlike to sometimes lower yourself to do things that you find unpleasant. As long as you do such things with dignity, you'll be a Felinist. Remember, when you're a cat, you treat everything as a kind of ballet. Sure, there will be times when you have to shit in a litter box, but if you can do it with delicacy and style, you will be a cat.'

The staff all laughed and clapped, and the meeting broke up on a cheerful note. They were all eager to be more like cats, to spend time with cats, and to convince their customers to send Casper money so they, too, could be like cats.

Chloe unlocked the front door and welcomed the customers who were already lining up outside.

9. Cats are hunters

Deep, unbroken concentration, a willingness to conceal and deceive when necessary, an unerring ability to focus on the target and deliver the final blow without mercy – these are the hallmarks of the hunter and the instinctive qualities of every cat. When you can stalk your prey with brutal efficiency and heartless equanimity, you can call yourself a cat.

Casper

The first fortnight of Cat Life was deliriously successful. The cats entertained, delighted and enchanted the customers, and the free use of computers and televisions to watch videos and flick through photos of cats drew a lot of otherwise bored and listless people. Almost all of the staff, whose agenda was to recruit new followers to Felinism, turned out to be superb hunters, and they brought in a lot of prey. The star performers, though, were Buffy and Misty, two different but complementary personalities who shared innate feline charisma, otherworldly beauty and an unflinching killer instinct.

Both were exquisite to look at, lithe and sensual in their

movements, and utterly irresistible when they set their minds to it. Buffy was a gorgeous blonde whose hair seemed to glow around her like a halo, and her narrow face with large almond eyes was dusted in a fine, delicate gossamer down, so that she seemed to have an ever-changing texture. A human movement student at university, she was an accomplished athlete who could dance, jump, run and fight with electrifying grace when she wanted to. But she was just as magnetic sitting still, looking into the distance with a wistful gaze and an apparently empty mind.

Misty was more of a free spirit, a nomad who wandered the world in search of inspiration and excitement, and everyone who met her was impressed by her complete lack of affectation. She was natural and casual, appearing carefree about everything, but like the good cat she was, she could switch on rigid deliberation when the mood took her, and then she became positively dangerous. Misty's thick, lustrous mane was a curious shade of blue-grey – no doubt the only part of her that was not completely natural – and her eyes seemed to be almost the same shade beneath heavy, usually blue-tinted lids. Her face was more oval and her nose longer and more defined than Buffy's, and while one would not compare the two in beauty, each was in her own right stunning – and well aware of the attraction she exerted on everyone they encountered.

Individually, they were formidable, but as a team Misty and Buffy were unstoppable. They charmed, cajoled and enticed customers into believing that just by taking home the free literature and tuning in to a few of Casper's free YouTube lectures, anyone could become as catlike as they were. Buffy had an incredible memory for faces and names, and whenever she spotted a returning customer, she cosied up to them with shameless effrontery, which they lapped up.

'Hi, Georgia,' she would beam almost the instant they came in. 'You came back!'

The customer would generally grin shyly and nod at the very least, and many were plainly overjoyed that this stunning young lady remembered them. She would usher them to a table or booth and, if the customer nodded agreement, would bring a house cat over and place it on their lap. This put the customer even more at ease, and opened them further to Buffy's subtle seduction.

'You are such a natural with Piper,' she would say. 'In fact, you're a bit of a cat yourself, aren't you?'

The customer would blush and smile, and pet the cat with gentle urgency.

'Look at you two; you could be sisters. Piper feels your felinity, and she's revelling in it. Last time you were here, you had a flat white and a piece of carrot cake – can I get you the same?'

Again the customer would flush with grateful pride that they had made such an impression on Buffy, and nod with helpless agreement. By that time, Buffy always knew that the catch was in the bag. She would walk away looking like she'd just licked the cream, and the customer would watch her supple retreat with warmth and empathy, and often more than a little bit of lust.

Returning with the order, Buffy would bring a sheaf of brochures and a free DVD with her and put them on the table. 'You know, you should consider joining our cat lovers' group,' she'd say.

'Oh, I don't know,' the customer usually said. 'I love cats, but I don't really want to join a group.'

'Oh, it's not a group as such. It's more like an online friendship thing, just sharing your cat experiences with others who love cats as much as you do. And the benefits include learning how being more like a cat can help you in life. Just watch the video or read the free stuff, and let's talk more next time you come in.'

The customer almost always came back within a day or two, intrigued by Casper's message and attracted by the idea that Buffy had taken a personal interest in them. From there she would invite them to a free session after hours as her personal guest, and the rest was mere formality. She wouldn't rest until she had made the kill, and once that was done, she walked away from the victim without looking back, moving on to the next target.

Misty's approach was much more free and easy. She acted like it didn't matter to her one way or another – a classic cat response – but intimated that she would think less of the customer if they didn't at least watch the DVD and then attend the free session. The very indifference she showed was almost always enough to drag the customer into her trap, and again the only thing that remained was to wrap the deal up.

In the first fortnight alone, these two managed to get over a dozen attendees to the first monthly free session, and over half were soon upgraded to Level Two members, committing to a monthly payment that was orders of magnitude higher than that extracted from Level One members.

10. Cats are divine

Why is it that five thousand years ago, our ancestors worshipped cats? It's because they recognised that cats possess much more power than the current generation projects. Cats made humans what they are today, and I can prove it to you if you join us and graduate to the upper levels of Felinism. Then you will worship them the way I do. When you accept that cats are divine, some of that divinity will become part of you.

Casper

'Welcome Felinists, welcome all,' said Chloe. She was glowing with pride and anticipation as she surveyed her audience. The Cat Life Centre had closed for the evening and the cats had all been put to bed, but all of Chloe's staff were there, along with almost two dozen Level One Felinists who were about to take the leap to Level Two commitment. Everyone in the room was as full of expectation and enthusiasm as the beaming young woman before them.

'You're here because you have all seen and experienced the benefits of being more like a cat. You've gained confidence, inner beauty, poise and just a little bit of mystery by following the teachings of Casper White. You've seen that Felinism is more than just an idea; it's a complete philosophy, an approach to life that gives you the tools to face any challenge, and the self-assurance to enjoy the victories that come with being as pure, as positive and as smart as a cat. Tonight, I am going to give you a little of the historical background to Felinism, and I hope to excite you enough to encourage you to take the next step and become a Level Three Felinist. As a Level Three myself, I can tell you that Casper has discovered the fundamental truth of what it is to be a human being, and of just how much we owe the last five thousand years of astounding growth and development to our relationship with cats. When you advance to Level Three, you will learn the full, enlightening reality of Felinism, and it will prepare you for a glorious future.

'Now, I am getting ahead of myself because I am so passionate about this, so let's take a step back. As Level One Felinists, you've been studying ways in which you can become more like a cat, interacting with cats of all personalities and outlooks whenever possible, and seeing how being more like a cat has changed the lives of so many people all over the world.

'Level Two is your introduction to the scientific and deeper philosophical background to Felinism. It's proof that cats and humans have an unbreakable connection that spans millennia and mirrors the advance of our civilisation. It's the beginning of Casper's divine truth, and it will change the way you see our world. Are you ready?'

Collective, eager agreement rang out from the crowd. Even Rex, standing at the back, was impatient to hear more.

He was beginning to believe he was becoming part of something special.

'Okay, I want you to think about the past.' Chloe's face was clear and her eyes were bright, and there was a hypnotic sensuality in her voice. 'Cast your mind back to the most amazing, successful and accomplished civilisation in human history: that of the ancient Egyptians. We still don't know how they built their pyramids, how they crafted their enormous temples and how they grew from being nomadic illiterates to take such great leaps forward in mathematics, science, art and culture that we are still finding out new things about them and their achievements.

'But we know that they did those things, because a lot of what they built and discovered still exists. And if you look carefully into the process – as Casper has done – you will see what took the Egyptians out of the desert and taught them to become the farmers, the inventors and discoverers, the artisans and the monumental city builders that they became. Cats.

'Before the Egyptians emerged to create their incomparable metropolises, to invent the first written languages, to reach for the sky and to change the future of humans, *Homo sapiens* was just another dumb, aimless species wandering around the planet trying to survive. The change that came about in that short time between about five and ten thousand years ago is so profound, so broad and central to who we are today, it's fair to say that before then, human beings as we know them didn't even exist.

'So, what changed? Cats came into our lives and created the species we became. And because of that, because they were there for the change and knew what had wrought it, the Egyptians worshipped cats. They venerated them and made harming them a serious crime, because they knew how important cats were to their society, to their very civilisation. Cats protected the grain stores from the pests and vermin that would steal or contaminate them – rats, mice, mongooses and so on – and they provided companionship and beauty. But that's just the headline; the real story is much deeper.

'When cats first came along, human beings were in reality just apes who could barely speak and who scrabbled around in the dirt. They met this vastly superior species, and the cats spoke to them. Not out loud, of course – please don't giggle, Rex, it doesn't do you any credit to be stupidly cynical.' Rex, who had been making great progress in becoming more like a cat but found the notion of talking cats frankly ludicrous, looked chagrined.

'You think it's silly that I think cats can talk to us with their minds, Rex? You're the ignorant one, because it doesn't take much to see that even today, cats find it easy to exert power over people. The great shame is that cats have lost a lot of their former mental potency, and as a consequence are not always revered as the formidable beings that they are. But even cats of the newest generation – today's kittens – have an irresistible, charismatic magic about them. Their capacity for projecting their thoughts and compelling humans to serve them – even though it has waned since the days of the Egyptians – is unparalleled in the animal world. We've talked about this before: the way a cat can command your attention, demand your services great and small. They've trained us to take away their bodily wastes, for god's sake. They routinely have us opening doors, waving toys at them for their amusement, patting them, brushing them, feeding them at their whim. And they give us virtually nothing in return. They don't work for us the way horses and dogs do. They don't ply us with affection or feed us with eggs or milk. They are the only domesticated creatures in our orbit that are there purely because they want to be. They have, in effect, made us their pets, although they allow us to believe that it's the other way around. Sure, they give us a purr every now and then, or the leftovers from a successful hunt. But in every important way, they have the upper hand in the relationship, and they know it.

'Just imagine how powerful they were ten thousand years ago, before the long decline in their ascendancy, brought on by the indolence that comes from being the objects of worship. Because that's what happened – they became so used to being feted, fed, cosseted and caressed that they got lazy and forgot just who they are. Or were.

'The first cats spoke to the minds of the pre-civilisation humans, and they told them what they needed to do to become a more dominant, a more stable and a more productive society – one worthy of serving cats. And they did this quite simply. They implanted in the humans' minds the possibility of storing food for lean times. They gave them the idea of not just gathering wild food and storing it, but of cultivating crops so they would have choices around what they ate, and consistency of supply. The leisure to enrich our human minds through enquiry was a happy by-product of this change, and the most consequential. Suddenly, people lived in one place all year round, and they didn't have to spend their entire time scrabbling for food and shelter. It changed us humans from wandering fools to fixed, focused achievers.

'Now, I can see some of you are asking, why would cats do this? What help was it to them if humans achieved all that? There's much more to it, which you will learn when you are initiated into Level Three Felinism, but I've already hinted at one answer. Cats knew that rats and mice eat grains. And as we're all aware, cats are born hunters. They love nothing more than to stalk, capture, torture and eat or abandon the carcasses of birds, rodents and small mammals. They understood that if they arranged it so humans grew and stored grains and other foods, these storehouses would attract their favourite prey. They gave humans the idea, and instilled in them the technical knowledge necessary to create these happy hunting grounds. We don't know just how they did it, but it's probable that cats somehow projected into the minds of their human companions images of structures, tools and materials, rather than telling them in so many words telepathically. In acting on these images – almost inspired dreams, if you will – the Egyptians discovered mathematics, building skills, architecture and farming, and so much more. All so they could, among other things, build smorgasbords for cats.

'Why didn't the cats cut out the middleman and do this for themselves? Because cats work with their minds. They're not suited physically or philosophically to manual labour. They needed something, or someone, with a reasonable level of dexterity – a species possessed of potential intelligence and an industrious nature – to do the work for them. Humans were most apt candidates. They had good-sized brains, and their senses were well developed. They'd even demonstrated some innate creativity in making and using tools before cats gave them the intellectual leg-up they needed to go the next step. But it was cats who provided that inspiration.

'Humans, of course, quickly adopted the cats' ideas as their own, and kept on growing their abilities. As time went on, the humans came to believe they were the smart ones and that cats were just pets, and the relationship kind of turned on its head. Over the course of thousands of years, humans have gradually lost their reverence for cats, and many of the cats' powers of projection and direction have wasted away. Today's cats are nowhere near as adept at controlling and instructing us as they were, even though they're still pretty damn good at ordering us about. In any case, their loss of power doesn't change how it all began. That's what brought us to where we are today.

'It took the mind of a man who was born to see cats in their pure, Egyptian form to discover this. Casper White has always seen the truth in and around cats, and through the Church of Felinism, he has shared that truth with us.

'Casper's logic is inescapable. Cats created human beings to serve them, and the first generations did just that. The ancient Mesopotamians and Egyptians who developed and spread civilisation worshipped cats, because they knew that without cats, *Homo sapiens* would still be scratching around for berries and swatting wildebeest on the head.

'That's why we Felinists today worship cats. We understand that we owe our present and our future to them, and that even though their powers have dissipated over the centuries, they will one day rediscover their true strength, and we humans, who arrogantly believe that we were born to rule, will be put back in our place. When that happens, the Felinists among us will be the exceptional people. We will be recognised as the ones who gave cats the opportunity to regain their pre-eminence, and we will be rewarded.

'In the meantime, we benefit from living and thinking more like cats. The more we know them, the more we are like them, the greater we become, and the greater the distance between us and ordinary humans. For – make no mistake, my friends – you are already extraordinary humans, and you are headed for greatness because you have chosen Felinism.

'Felinism teaches us not just about cats, but about ourselves. It allows us to model our behaviour on that of the most elegant, intelligent and advanced species on the planet, which also happens to be the most beautiful. Look at us, surrounded by these living examples of where we came from, where we are going and how we should live.' The cats had all gone to bed, but the appreciative crowd knew what Chloe was talking about, and most of them beamed and nodded hearty agreement.

'So, welcome,' finished Chloe with a bright, beatific smile. 'Welcome to Level Two Felinism, and to a brilliant, blissful, feline future!'

11. Cats are possessive

Just because a cat appears to have discarded a plaything, its ownership status does not change. That ownership can be reasserted at any time, and serves as a reminder to others that the cat is in charge of its own destiny. When you can treat your toys and baubles, as well as your relationships, like pawns in a lifelong chess game, you will be more like a cat.

Casper

The meeting went on for some time as Chloe spruiked the various videos, books, pamphlets and merchandise the new acolytes would need to own and study before they could truly embody the greatness and significance of cats, and call themselves Level Two Felinists. She wound up proceedings by answering questions and providing more detail about the divinity of cats – without, of course, giving away any of the information restricted to Level Three Felinists.

Although critical to a complete understanding of Felinism, and a necessary step in accepting the ultimate truth of it, Level Three intelligence could not be given to just anyone. Only those that proved their worthiness through dedication to study, an ongoing pattern of catlike behaviour, adherence to the tenets of Felinism, and most importantly a generous ongoing financial contribution to the church, could be admitted to this level.

Chloe felt certain that most of the people in the room would go on to become Level Three believers. They were all impressed and excited by her speech, and – crucially – the majority of them had that unique quality of blindness to their insecurities so important to successful indoctrination into a life-changing creed. They thought they were learning to be more catlike, without realising that for the organisation their most salient and enduring characteristic was their capacity to act like sheep. Most of all, every one of them possessed the attribute that most counted towards qualifying for induction into Level Three: the capacity and willingness to keep on paying into the church coffers. Chloe loved them for it, and she was sure that when they were all much more cattish than they were at that moment, they would thank her for it. Meanwhile, Casper would thank her for helping the organisation to grow and his influence to spread.

As she finished the formal part of the evening, Chloe invited the guests to stay on for a drink and a chat, and every one remained. Like a graceful ghost, she glided through the little groups that had formed, patting arms and bestowing encouraging glances, and anyone she touched or smiled at felt special. She noticed that Misty, the free-spirited hunter, was monopolising Rex's time. From where Chloe watched through hooded eyes, it appeared that almost everything Rex said seemed to be either hilarious or enthralling, because Misty alternated between emanating a curious tinkling laughter and looking deeply and gravely into his eyes. There was also an inordinate amount of hair flicking, arm touching and lip licking going on, which Chloe found as inelegant as it was obvious.

Unfortunately, she got bogged down with a Dalkeith matron, who had too much time on her hands and too little to occupy her mind and drain her bank accounts, and had become infatuated with the precepts and purported benefits of Felinism. Chloe couldn't abandon this lady, because she showed every sign of becoming a substantial benefactor, but as she answered inane questions regarding the finer points of feline behaviour, her eyes were locked on Misty and Rex. And in her mind, she was preparing the scathing dressing-down that she would give Misty for failing to mingle with the other guests. Rex might be a paid-up Level Two, but he was also, she would remind Misty, just another hired hand, and not worthy of the attention.

Chloe's impulse was to advise Misty that she might be better employed elsewhere – at some reggae-loving, dreadlock -growing, herbally aromatic commune, for instance. But Misty was such a prolific recruiter of novice Felinists, and an accomplished waiter to boot – she shifted a lot of muffins – that such a suggestion might prove hasty.

At last the chatter of the Dalkeith drone slowed and then stopped, and the lady excused herself. Chloe tore her eyes away from Rex and Misty and fixed her brightest smile on the lady. She would love to see her again any time, and would adore spending more time with her discussing the minutiae of feline conduct, and was tremendously grateful for the lady's presence at this little soiree, etcetera. To be honest, she wasn't listening to what she was saying, but she knew she was saying it with perfectly assumed sincerity and the most dazzling of smiles, and she knew the lonely lady was buying it by the truckload.

They air-kissed and the lady departed, and Chloe stalked over to where Misty and Rex were still enjoying their animated conversation.

'Rex, darling, I am so glad you could make it.'

In an instant, Misty ceased to exist and Rex's eyes took on that shine reserved for Chloe. She smiled a knowing, not quite gloating smile at Misty, and the latter, like a kitten that has been cuffed by her mother, looked chastened and admiring at the same time. She knew she had been bested, and she understood that to enter into a contest now would be futile. She melted away with a rueful smile and quick shake of the head; every time she thought she was a cat, Chloe came and showed her that she still had much to learn.

Chloe, noting Misty's swift withdrawal, made a mental note to retain the rebuke she'd already composed, in case she should need it later. There was no longer any call for it.

'Oh, Chloe, you were awesome,' said Rex. He looked like he wanted to take her hands in his own, but instead his meaty appendages were left flopping around like dying fish. 'The way you explained it, it all makes so much sense now.'

'Maybe you'd like to tell me what you most liked about it while you buy me dinner?'

'That would be great.' He couldn't agree fast enough.

He was gratified that she had either forgotten or forgiven his disruptive chortle over that business of cats talking telepathically to people, blissfully unaware that she had chosen to overlook his otherwise unacceptable behaviour – for now – only because she had caught Misty flirting with him.

'Just let me shoo these people away,' said Chloe. 'Then you and I can go and have a nice quiet bite.' She snapped her teeth together so they made a soft, hot click in Rex's ear, and his face went red and his blood boiled just a little. He couldn't wait.

12. Cats make statements

Every now and then, a cat will do something unexpected, dramatic and apparently pointless; like shitting on your bed, swatting an expensive vase off a table, or jumping up onto your lap to deliver some gratuitous affection. They do it to remind you that they are fearless, fanciful and capable of anything. Be like a cat – make a statement today.

Casper

After they were seated and Chloe had ordered an expensive drink, she fixed him with a penetrating stare but said nothing. Rex tried to hold her gaze but couldn't bear it for more than a few seconds, looking away shy and confused. Eventually, he had to look back at her, and she was still regarding him with that cool, hard glare.

He had no idea what he'd done or how to fix it, so he looked around the room for help. None was forthcoming. The silence was becoming torture to him, and though he knew that if he were the one to break it he would lose, he couldn't stand it any longer.

He looked at the table, bit his lower lip to stop it quivering, and said, 'I'm sorry I laughed. It was rude and ignorant, and I'll never do it again. I understand what you meant now, but at the time it sounded funny.'

At first Chloe shook her head dismissively, then she sat back and arched her shoulders, as though relaxing. Or flexing. Still she said nothing; still she kept up that unsettling stare.

Again, he reached his breaking point with astonishing speed. 'What?' he asked in desperation.

She leaned forward as though about to impart an important principle. 'Don't be a settler, Rex,' she said.

A soft groan escaped him. 'Oh, god,' he said. 'Are we back to the dog business again?'

She chuckled like an evil mastermind. He was all hers. 'I said settler, sweetie, not setter. As in, don't settle for a little slut like Misty.'

Rex was thrown. He tried to picture that sweet, spontaneous hippy as a slut, but he couldn't. Surely Chloe was exaggerating for effect. But somewhere in the back of his mind a light went on, and it said *Chloe Is Jealous* in blinking neon. He felt as though he should defend Misty, but he didn't want to break this new spell. What could he do?

'You really think she's a slut?' he said.

'She was all over you,' she replied. 'What does that tell you?'

Ouch. That hurt.

'But you're better than that, sweetie.'

Okay, that eased the pain a bit. He felt bad for Misty, but fuck her; this was about him and Chloe. He tried to shrug the whole thing off with a grin.

'I was just being nice because she works for you,' he said.

'I was practising being a cat. Rowwrr.' He twirled his fingers like sausage shaped claws in such a bad imitation of a cat that Chloe had to laugh.

'You have quite a long way to go, darling, but you'll get there,' she lied. 'I'm very pleased you've become a permanent member of our group.'

Knowing it would be impolitic to admit that he'd joined the group to be closer to her, Rex extemporised. He wished he'd thought up a more plausible response earlier, but he hadn't – he'd been genuinely engaged with Misty and thought her quite beautiful, so his mind hadn't been working very well, anyway – so he said the first thing that came to him.

'I really want to learn to be more like a cat. I can see how your feline qualities help to make you the wonderful success you are, and I'd like to be more like you.'

Bing! Correct answer. Chloe's eyes lit up like a Roman candle, and her smile was authentic. All of a sudden, everything was coming up Rexy.

'So, tell me what you loved about our meeting,' she said. 'And don't leave a single compliment out.'

For the next twenty minutes – allowing for gaps in which she ordered various drinks and dishes – Chloe listened in rapt attention as Rex regurgitated what she had said almost word for word, as though he had taken it all to heart and made it his new mantra. She gently corrected him when he screwed it up, clicked her tongue approvingly when he got it right, and lapped up every bit of lavish praise he heaped on her, which was a lot. A bystander might have thought he was a brickie rather than a carpenter, because he was laying it on with a trowel.

By the time he had exhausted his supply of memorised Felinisms, tributes and accolades, Chloe was both chuffed and chilled. It was as though he'd been patting her special spot for ages, and she was almost hypnotised by it all. There was a far-away, dreamy look in her eye, and it took her a while to awaken fully. She had to admire Rex's conscientious assimilation of everything she had said, and she hoped that everyone else in the crowd had come away as well programmed. She picked at her seafood pasta while, suddenly ravenous, Rex tucked into the big juicy bangers and mash that had been cooling before him for the last five minutes of his homily. He was in heaven.

So of course the hammer had to come down. She started by acknowledging Rex's attentiveness and encouraged him to continue on in his Felinist studies with the same enthusiasm, and his spirits soared. It had to come, though. He could sense it getting closer as her praise got warmer, and then she said it: the B word. 'But...I'm afraid, my darling, that you're not convincing as a cat. And here's why...'

His personal hygiene, dress sense, the loudness with which he spoke, the state of his car with all those empty iced coffee cartons that had so quickly repopulated the footwells, his hair, his susceptibility to the flattering attentions of little sluts like Misty (who didn't have his best interests at heart the way Chloe did), and much, much more were addressed in a lengthy, searing critique of his character, appearance and prospects. It was merciless. Relentless. Inescapable. Uncompromising.

When at last she had finished, and Rex's big mushy heart was a mess of torn and bloodied tissue somewhere on the floor, he was shattered. He felt as though he didn't even deserve to get up from the table and go to the counter to pay for their meals. But somehow, he found the strength, and came back to find Chloe preening herself with the help of a small compact mirror. She barely gave him a second glance, and while she strode out to his car with the air of one who has just conquered an entire nation, he trudged behind, a disconsolate fragment of a man.

The whole drive home, Chloe was the only one to speak. 'It's for your own good, you know darling,' was all she said, with crisp efficiency. And she patted his knee proprietarily, which cheered him up a bit, but he was longing to get home and curl up on his mattress. He had a feeling his blanket would get a good chewing that night.

He pulled up outside Chloe's house and waited for her to get out and walk away without looking back, leaving him to his misery.

'Why don't you come inside, Rexy?' she said. There was an odd, husky tone in her voice. It was as though all that savagery had somehow heated her up. Rex may have been a sad shell of brokenness, but he wasn't a complete idiot. He jumped out of that car like he had just arrived at the beach. There followed a magical hour in which Chloe seduced him with delicious thoroughness, treating him like some sort of king and making herself a slave to his every whim. It was beautiful, surreal and, in the case of the final act, surprisingly satisfying, at least as far as she was concerned. It was the culmination of a lifelong dream for Rex, and he wasn't sure if he should just up and die right then and there, because life could not, surely, get any better. And yet, if he somehow clung on to this post-ecstatic life, maybe, just maybe, there would be more of this in store.

Lying back in ecstasy, he mused on how this whole event had been brought about by the delightful expedient of having a warm conversation with a very attractive young lady other than Chloe. Who knew, perhaps the future held further opportunities to use his charms on other young ladies as a means of stirring Chloe to similar possessive actions. He wondered if he really was becoming a cat.

Chloe's voice cut through his misty reverie. 'You'd better go home, Rexy darling. I have a big day tomorrow.' She didn't kiss him goodbye, though god knows he went in for it and was left hanging like a big lippy mask on a wall.

He let himself out.

13. Cats are spontaneous

Cats don't like to be predictable. Being arbitrary makes them harder to pin down, more of a challenge to read, and more fun to be around. And sometimes what appears to be an impulsive action by a cat can, in light of later developments, be revealed to be a cunning piece of planning. Never underestimate the power of a cat's foresight, and cultivate the same impulses in yourself.

Casper

Lying in bed after Rex had left, considering whether she had the energy to get up and wash the sheets straight away, Chloe contemplated what had just happened. She hadn't intended to throw him a bone like that, but then again, she hadn't intended to harangue him quite so ferociously at dinner. And when she had, she'd felt sorry for him and figured that he needed a little incentive to stay devoted to her. For all his faults, Rex was a true and unquestioning friend, as well as a very handy accessory to have around at times, and that business with Misty had prompted her to reel him in a little.

She decided not to wash the sheets. They smelled of Rex,

and Rex smelled strong and masculine. How could she not be more than a little fond of someone so loyal, talented and, most surprisingly of all, sexy? For an act of whimsy that she expected to unfold as a dreary, malodorous chore, the way he had so thoroughly ravished her and the unimagined rapture he had delivered had been a spectacular way to finish off a successful night. She hadn't realised just how hungry she had been for a bit of man flesh, and she was thrilled that Rex had performed so impressively.

It made her wonder. He had claimed to have missed her, but it was obvious he'd been out there practising his technique on someone. Quite likely, he'd have practised it on Misty if she hadn't stepped in. She resolved to keep a tighter leash on him, because she needed his manly skills and strength around the centre, and she was quite sure he would become a long-term contributor to the cause. If she was being honest with herself, it was difficult to imagine life without Rex at her beck and call. Besides, in Casper's absence, he was as good as any man to meet her needs. Better to give him a little treat now and then to keep his interest kindled than to have to find some other Tom or Dick to harry.

In Casper's absence… That had reminded her of Him. He of the clear eyes, the perfect straight white hair, shapely aquiline nose and irresistible ways. The most accomplished human feline on the planet, a man so naturally catlike she wondered what he had been like when he was a kitten.

Casper had taught Chloe so much, but more than that, he'd shown her what she could be and then given her the opportunity to become it. Her time in the States had been a wonderful mixture of learning, laughing, working harder than she ever had before but enjoying the rewards so much more intensely and, most of all, becoming part of something much bigger than she had believed could exist. They were creating a new religion, for Christ's sake. Even more amazing, she was bringing it to Australia. What an incredible demonstration of Casper's trust in her, and what an honour.

She hoped and swore that she would never let him down. She saw a distant future in which they were together, at the head of their global church, helping ordinary people to be more like cats and to reap the benefits of their felinity. And then, one day long, long in the future, it would happen. The breathtaking event that Casper had foreseen would occur, and they would be transported to another place, a new level of perfection.

Ah, but she was getting ahead of herself. She was still the only person in Australia to have been initiated into Level Three Felinism, and there was much to be done to prepare the way for that glorious tomorrow. She was drifting off to sleep, and as she slid into that delicious pre-slumber state where any-thing seems possible, she saw Casper's head floating above her, his hands reaching out to her, his voice calling her...

And then she was wide awake, because her bloody computer was making a weird bubbling, gurgling sound as though it was trying to sing underwater. Wait! That was the Skype tone. Who could be calling her at this ridiculous hour? Probably one of the office minions from San Diego, issuing some new order or demanding yet another onerous new reporting regime. Selfish arseholes – she would tear them a new one.

She got out of bed and smacked the light switch, and went to the open laptop. The face on the caller's avatar quickened her heart and re-heated her loins. It was a gorgeous Prussian blue cat in stately repose, a haughty smirk on its face. It must be Him! She tried to make herself look presentable, brushing the hair out of her eyes and attempting to compose her face, fearful that if she took too long, he would hang up. As soon as she could, she clicked the answer icon, and waited, breathless, for his face to appear, wanting to throw herself at the machine and hug it, but aware that to do so would not be very catlike.

Casper's sunny, smiling face filled the screen and her heart, and the heat in her veins jumped another notch.

'Helloooo,' she purred.

'Hey, doll,' he said. His smile faded a touch and he looked concerned, as he would if a fly had landed next to his food or he felt a distant draught from an open door – a fleeting, easily dismissed concern. 'Did I wake you up? Shit, sorry.'

'I was awake,' Chloe said. It wasn't a complete lie – she had been awake until only a short time before, and she hadn't yet been fully asleep. 'Anyway, it doesn't matter, because here we are.' She smiled brightly.

'Here we are indeed,' he said, and took a sip of his milk. He always had a long, cold glassful on hand, unless it was beer o'clock. 'I just want you to know I'm excited at what you're doing over there in the West. It looks like you're making terrific progress.'

'Oh yeah, it's going great,' she said. 'We've got a good number of Level Twos already, and by the end of next month, I'm sure we'll have a lot more. People love the cats, they love your videos and writings, and they love to discover the cat within themselves. It really helps them grow.' Her face clouded a little. 'Is everything alright on the business side? I'm sending all the accounts and stuff to Jasmine.'

'Everything's fine,' said Casper. 'You're doing a fabulous job, and there are no complaints from the accounts team or the business team. I only called to say how happy we are with the way it's going. In fact, it's going so well that I want to expand the Aussie operation a bit quicker than was first planned. It's time we hit the market on the east coast.'

'Wow.' Chloe was stunned. 'That's awesome.'

'Even better, I think I want to get this thing rolling myself,' said Casper. 'I'm coming home – I'll see you in a week or two.'

14. Cats are frisky

It's not all solemn contemplation and dark predation with cats. Sometimes they like to just let it all hang out and do what comes naturally. When a cat is feeling frivolous and frisky, it's best if you're available for whatever takes their fancy. Because there's nothing quite as fiery as a frustrated feline.

Casper

Far below, the blue Pacific sparkled like an endless lake, and the unending hum of the engines was only just audible beneath the gentle tones of the Al Stewart track filtering through Casper's earphones. He turned from the window and stood in the doorway of his first-class suite to look around. The cabin was only about half full, and most people travelled with their suite doors open unless they were sleeping. Everyone was occupied watching movies or reading, and one or two appeared to be working. The exception was Paris, top cat of PR for the Church of Felinism. Casper liked to surround himself with Australians – he trusted them more than he did Americans – and Paris had been with him the longest of any of his troupe. She was dozing in her open suite, her seat reclined but not flattened to a bed, with her face mask on, her mouth very slightly open and a little pink tip of pointed tongue peeping out of the opening. Her sharp blonde hair was arranged with surprising structure around her on a plush pillow, and she looked supremely comfortable.

Casper licked the back of his left wrist and rubbed it behind his ear thoughtfully. Sure, it was an affectation, but he had been affecting it for so long that it came naturally to him, and people who saw him do it for the first time usually thought it adorable and oh-so catlike. Truth be told, he wasn't feeling awfully cattish right then. The first-class seats might be comfortable and infinitely more adjustable than the ones in the back of a plane – or on the lower floor of this fancy double decker jet – but his long limbs couldn't find comfort, and his mind was uncharacteristically busy. The trip to Australia had been brought forward in the plans, and he was a bit nervous about going home for the first time in such a long time. But the rumours about the IRS had persisted, and if there was any truth in them, he didn't want to be in the States if and when the speculated raid took place.

Then again, it would be nice to be home. He wasn't going to stop in Sydney and see the family; the plan was to get a connecting flight to Perth and kick the thing off with a media and local A-list event at the Subiaco Cat Life Centre. Paris had briefed Chloe on the need for a press contingent to be at Perth Airport when he arrived, and they had scheduled the Cat Life Centre bash for a couple of days later.

Taking off his earphones and dropping them on his seat, Casper sauntered back towards the business-class cabin, where Coco and Yuki were slumming it. Yuki was curled up with a thick strand of black hair over her face like a tail, and Coco was stretched out watching a movie on her screen. As soon as she saw Casper, she hit the pause button and jumped up to join him. Together they went to the bar at the rear of the cabin, and Casper ordered a couple of drinks.

Casper clinked glasses with her and stared into her eyes, sending a shudder of delight echoing through her whole body. 'Are you looking forward to seeing Australia?' he asked. Coco was a stunning deep brunette with long, languid features and a dreamy smile. She wasn't the smartest person in Casper's entourage, but in many respects, she was the most innately feline. And she was a tiger in the sack, which counted for a lot in Casper's estimation. He liked to keep a few tigers around, even though he would have disputed a direct family link between tigers and other 'big cats' and the domestic cats he worshipped. 'Yes, they're made from the same basic stuff,' he would say to anyone who mentioned the connection. 'But that doesn't make them the same. Humans share a lot of DNA with pigs – does that make us directly related? Of course not. Although I have known a few hogs in my time…'

'Oh, I am so pleased to be going to Australia,' Coco said. 'I can't imagine what it'll be like.' A native of San Diego, Coco was like most of her compatriots in that she couldn't find Australia – or almost any other country except perhaps Canada or Mexico – on a map, and had no idea what happened there. She was going in completely blind, and it would probably be a surprise to her to learn that Australians speak a brand of English.

'Well, we'll be going straight over to Perth,' said Casper. 'And I'm told that the climate and the lifestyle is a lot like where we've just come from – your hometown, San Diego. There are a few more people and a lot less armed forces living there, and of course not everyone has a gun, but essentially it's the same.

And since the US has never bombed Australia and only ever once overthrown its government, we Aussies like Americans.'

Coco adored Casper and believed everything he said. She sipped on her Mai Tai and nodded, batting her long black lashes prettily.

'You remember Chloe?' said Casper. 'She's been over there for a couple of months setting up the first Australian Cat Life Centre, so I figured it's time we went over there and helped out.'

'You're so thoughtful.' Coco remembered Chloe as a rival for the chief tomcat's affections, and was less than overjoyed that she was coming back into the frame, but she was far too felinely circumspect to let that slip. She had Casper there with her then, and if she played her cards right, she might even get to help him join the mile-high club. She could already feel her claws in his back, and suddenly he could feel it too. He was pleased Coco had so effectively taken his mind off his potential problems and relocated his focus to his groin. They didn't need to speak; they both knew what was up. They finished their drinks and Casper led Coco back to the first-class cabin, where he closed the door of his suite behind them.

15. Cats are charming

When a cat wants to be your friend, they don't give you any right of refusal. They will use every artifice in their extensive arsenal to flatter, cajole and disarm you, and they won't give up until you're completely charmed and unconditionally theirs for life. Be as charming as a cat.

Casper

Even with its alluring distractions and diversions, the flight was fifteen hours from Los Angeles to Sydney, followed by a four-hour wait at Sydney Airport and then a cross-continental trek to Perth. And though the first-class seats were a big help, Casper wasn't feeling his shiny best when they finally walked out of the domestic arrivals hall. He'd stopped to clean and preen once more in the bathroom near the baggage carousel so he would look fresher than he felt. That was a good thing, because Chloe had a sizeable press contingent waiting. Not exactly a pack of paparazzi, but we are talking about a town with a relatively small media presence – most of Perth's news, opinions and fashions are imported from much wiser heads in the east. For the assembled hacks, having first crack at this mysterious cat guru was something of a coup: an opportunity to show they could be as hard-hitting and probing as any of those smartarse eastern states wankers.

Casper walked out with his cream pants and cheese-cloth shirt looking remarkably crisp after such an arduous journey, his long, straight blonde hair jouncing in the gentle air-conditioned breeze, and his expression serene and superior.

It should be pointed out here that somewhere early in the twenty-first century, an unspoken agreement swept the media of Australia to primarily, if not exclusively, employ sexy young blonde ladies as television reporters. So the ranks of all media present were awash with sensationally svelte young goddesses either already standing before television cameras or hoping to be elevated to that station (from the lowly ranks of radio or press reporting) soon. When the gaggle of gorgeous correspondents clogging the arrival area saw Casper saunter-ing out with his retinue of Paris, Coco and Yuki following a respectful distance behind, their eyes popped and their instinct for the continuation of the species kicked in. Any thoughts of grilling this supposedly shadowy figure over his cult, his apparent penchant for employing chiefly attractive young women (wait, could this mean an opportunity?), and vague rumours of troubles with the IRS, all dissolved. Cameramen sighed, the one or two male reporters ground their teeth, and the ladies jostled to get closer.

Casper didn't want to stop for long – he was tired and wanted to get to a darkened hotel room as soon as possible, drink a large, cold Australian beer, and curl up for a nap – but he was gratified and entertained to see such an eye-catching press corps, and stayed longer than he'd planned. He smiled brightly, chuckled with carefree grace and posed naturally as the questions, mainly about his plans while in Perth, his famed feline qualities and the stellar success of his group – none dared call it a cult in his presence – flew. The lady reporters all strove to outdo each other with flattering questions that portrayed them in a fawning good light, and Casper obliged by looking each questioner directly in the eye and answering in the most engaging and charming way possible. You could almost hear the communal swoon every time he smiled, and the simpering laughs that accompanied his every joke were music to his ears.

Not everyone was impressed, though. Rex, for one. He'd been co-opted to drive a minibus for Casper's entourage, and from the moment he'd first seen the man he'd been jealous to the point of desperation. He could see the effect this fellow was having on almost everyone else in the building, including Chloe – and though he had to grudgingly admire the way Casper handled himself, he vowed never to fall under his spell. The other person to share Rex's distaste was one of the aforementioned and notably rare male reporters, a hard-bitten cynic by the name of Butch McNab.

Butch the Cult-Buster, as he was otherwise known, felt he could see straight through this shyster, and itched for the chance to prove it. But of course, it was impossible for him to get a question in while Casper was surrounded by this pack of appreciative correspondents, and it would probably have been precipitate to give away his animosity in such an admiring atmosphere. He quietly seethed in the background and made a vow of his own: to catch this cat in a trap.

After a good long while being witty, flicking his hair with delicious insouciance and distributing his abundant pheromones to the gallery, Casper called an end to the presser and strode off towards the carpark with his entourage trailing behind. Chloe and Casper rode in the limousine she had organised, while Rex was tasked with getting all the bags and baggage, including Paris, Yuki and Coco, into the minibus he had hired for the purpose. The girls were excited to be in a new city in a country they had only seen from airside so far, and they chattered all the way, peppering Rex with delightfully ingenuous questions like, 'Will we see kangaroos on the streets?' By the time they pulled into the city hotel Chloe had booked for them all, Rex had quite forgotten how much he'd instantly hated Casper, and could only remember how grateful he was that he'd brought these lovely young lasses with him. He figured he might enjoy Casper's stay after all.

16. Dogs are faithful

A dog will play with almost anything or anyone – they are terribly indiscriminate that way – but their first loyalty will always be to the one they think of as their master. This is one of the many ways in which they are inferior to cats – a cat's loyalty is always to itself, and cats understand that fidelity is something to receive rather than to give. Be more like a cat.

Casper

Airports, Rex mused to himself as he drove the van full of luggage and loveliness to the city, seem always to be located in the place least likely to present the visitor with an appealing or even mildly agreeable first impression. He knew this because he had once been to Melbourne, and several times had made the short hop to Bali with mates, to drink Bintang from an early to a late hour every day and dress exclusively in board shorts and a singlet. So he counted himself an expert in airports and travel.

But the nondescript streets on the road from Perth Airport, the standard, walled freeway, and then the streets with straggly trees and shabby houses between rows of gaudy shops didn't seem to bother Yuki, Coco and Paris. All three kept up a steady stream of chatter and catty laughter, seeming not to notice the cloudless April skies above or the colourless suburbs around them.

When they arrived at their hotel, part of a vast commercial and residential complex that would not have been out of place almost anywhere in the world – which means it held no architectural distinction at all – the three passengers expressed no surprise or extraordinary satisfaction at its appearance or impressiveness, just as they had offered no opinions of Perth during the short ride. To them, this was simply another city and another hotel, and Rex took this as a personal affront. However much they may criticise their home and complain about it, Perth people (or *Perth'uns*, as Rex always thought of them) are exceptionally proud of their sprawling coastal capital, and become disturbed and offended if visitors don't start throwing around superlatives about it from the moment they arrive.

He parked behind Casper's limo and the trio leapt out of the van with lithe self-assurance, strutting into the lobby like they owned it and leaving Rex behind to deal with their unbelievable volume of baggage. By the time he and several staff members had wrangled four trolleys packed with expensive bags into the lobby, there was no sign of Casper and Chloe, and Paris had disappeared as well. Only Coco and Yuki stood at the check-in counter, awaiting the return of their passports, which had been taken away for photocopying, and their room keys. Rex wandered up to them shyly.

'Where did Chloe and Casper go?'

Coco giggled and Yuki said, 'They had some stuff to do

upstairs. Stuff you hang the "Do Not Disturb" sign for, if you know what I mean.'

The smile that had been frozen on Rex's face since they'd left the airport disappeared, and his expression turned to one of morose disappointment. He looked beaten.

'Okay,' he said. 'I guess I'll see you later. Have a nice night.'

'Hey, slow down there, big boy,' said Yuki, catching his arm. 'You're not going anywhere without us. Come on upstairs while we shower, and then the three of us are going out on the town. You're going to show us how awesome Perth can be.'

Shepherding two scatty cat people around town – even a pair as gorgeous as these two – didn't appeal to Rex right then, but neither did going home to chew his blanket or play with his ball. He shrugged and followed them to the lift.

It wasn't quite the presidential suite – Casper and Chloe had that one – but the suite the girls shared was the biggest and most expensive hotel room Rex had ever been in. The large windows offered expansive views across the Swan River, just then sparkling gold in the lowering western sunlight, to the tight jumble of skyscrapers that marked the city's rather compact business centre. Over on their right, a round structure like a giant wicker basket glowed purple and white, and headlights twinkled up and down the roadways.

'Oh my god, it's gorgeous,' said Coco. Rex brightened, and his chest swelled with civic pride. 'So small and pretty,' added Yuki. Minor lessening of the chestal inflation.

'But what's that thing, and why is it glowing like that?' Coco was pointing at the wicker basket.

'That's the craypot,' Rex replied.

'The what?' Both girls looked stumped.

'The craypot,' he repeated. 'Don't you think it looks like an old-fashioned craypot?'

'Dude, I have no idea what you're talking about.'

He yukked like a yokel. 'Oh right. It's the local stadium, and there's a footy game on. Freo is playing, and that's why the lights are purple.'

'Footy? Freo?' Yuki wasn't sure he was speaking English any more. 'And what the hell is a craypot?'

'Ha ha, something you catch crayfish in, of course.' The two of them continued to look blank and were perhaps in danger of losing interest. 'You know, lobster? Don't worry; I'll explain it to you as we go. Footy too.' He picked up the remote control and switched the television on, flopping onto the couch and dropping his huge feet onto the expensive jarrah coffee table. 'Now go get showered or changed or whatever, and we can head off.'

He punched the button for the local channel showing the football game, and the girls went off to their separate bedrooms and bathrooms to prepare. As he watched the Fremantle Dockers getting flogged by Richmond, Rex thought about Chloe, no doubt copping a royal rogering from that pretty boy Casper right above him. It made his heart ache almost as much as every goal that the Tigers kicked against his beloved purple warriors. Still, he said to himself, trying to find the bright side, he was about to spend Saturday night out on the town with two stunning young visitors who would naturally see him as the local expert on anything he cared to discuss. It could be a fun evening.

A short while later, long legs, short skirts and tight, spangled blouses got between Rex and the television, and it was time to go. He had to admit the girls cleaned up very well indeed, and he was glad he'd put on his best black jeans and the floral shirt that Chloe loved so much but he thought was vaguely gay.

The valet brought the van up from the car park, which made Rex feel like a tycoon, and they headed off for the city. He took the long way so he could show the girls the scenic highlights of the city, namely a small, square harbour and a bell tower, and between pointing out Perth's architectural and engineering wonders, he tried to explain Australian rules football. He told them 'Ozzierools' is a game where thirty-six players run up and down a randomly shaped roundish field chasing an oval ball and beating the shit out of each other, introducing them to terms like ruck, rover, mark, holding the ball, green maggots, corks and hammies, much to their bewildered amusement. By the time he'd finished, the girls were no closer to under -standing the game or being convinced of Australians' sanity, but they were charmed by Rex's goofy affability and weird idiom, and found the big, shaggy bugger oddly appealing.

They were still laughing, and giving each other knowing looks about what might happen later, when Rex pulled into a busy car park that smelled of urine and kebabs. The entertainment hub of Northbridge was already humming.

The first item of business was food – Coco and Yuki were ravenous, they said – so they walked around looking for somewhere suitable to dine. To Rex's dismay, they ignored the steak bars, pizza joints and food halls in favour of a Japanese restaurant. He had no idea what to order, so he told the girls to choose, contenting himself with tucking into a Kirin Lager. The food, when it came, was all raw – some of it fish, and some of it something worse. It smelled like cat food, and the girls lapped it up, squealing with delight as they did so. He tasted a small, cubical lump of cold, grey flesh that he had been told was tuna but which tasted more like rubber soaked in ancient fish sauce, and ate no more. His earlier misery was beginning to make a comeback, and his mind kept returning to that accursed presidential suite, where Chloe and Casper were doubtless vigorously renewing their acquaintance for the third or fourth time, or at least munching on something edible like a big chunk of rare Angus.

The ordeal of dinner behind him, the increasingly sullen Rex followed the progressively more beautiful and noisy Coco and Yuki through the neon-bright streets looking for a bar that suited their tastes. This turned out to be a gay bar, in which loud music thumped and whumped without cease, glamorously dressed bodies of all genders pressed against each other in a crush of joy and sweat, and Rex stood out like a Baptist at a pride parade – in spite of his shirt. He longed for the relatively minor discomfort of the Japanese restaurant.

An hour later, the girls had danced and laughed and drank enough there and wanted to see something else. They hustled out onto the street, and Rex, fearful that the next destination would be as alien to him as the last two, took charge. 'Northbridge sucks,' he said with authority. 'Let's go to Freo.'

'Freo?'

'Weren't you listening to the footy explanation? The team is the town – Freo: Fremantle. It makes this place look cheap, and it's less crowded and noisy.' He thought, but didn't bother to add, that at least in Fremantle the blood and chunder wouldn't begin to flow until much later in the night. Here in Northbridge, at 10.30 the atmosphere was already beginning to simmer with the suggestion of imminent violence.

Walking through the gates in the limestone wall into the beer garden at the Norfolk Hotel, Rex began to feel like a king. Drinkers of all ages and stages of inebriation were casting appreciative looks at Yuki and Coco, and the girls were raving about how wonderful and quaint the port city was. He found them a table and got a round of drinks, and for a long while they sat and chatted, the girls turning away the approaches of besotted sots with cute rebuttals and sweet smiles. Now and then, Yuki or Coco would let some grinning fool join them for a few moments, but they weren't really hunting for conquests, merely toying with the prey before discarding it. It was funny and empowering, and Rex revelled in the envious looks he was getting from almost everyone in the pub. He relaxed and played the game with the two proud, beautiful young women, sipped his craft beer and forgot all about Chloe for a while.

When the pub closed at 1 a.m., they walked the short way down the now quiet Cappuccino Strip to a nightclub, but there was a long line out the door, and Yuki had begun to yawn and stretch every few minutes. Jetlag was starting to overtake enthusiasm. They went back to the hotel, and at the front door, Rex prepared to drop the girls off and go home alone, but Coco in particular wouldn't hear of it.

'Oh, Rexy, no,' she said. 'Yuki is half asleep already, but I'm wide awake. Won't you come and have a nightcap with me?' Eyelashes batted, lips curled and hair was flipped. Rex hesitated for about a nanosecond, but then thought of Chloe and Casper upstairs, sated and napping amongst a tangle of sheets and bodily fluids. He got out and handed the keys to the sleepy valet parking attendant. 'Put it on Mr White's tab.'

The three of them went upstairs and Yuki, having taken the hint, slipped off to her room. Coco poured herself a brandy and Rex a scotch, and beckoned him to the couch. He sat stiff and nervous as she pawed and petted him, stroked his shaggy hair and cooed softly about what a good boy he was, and kept his eyes locked straight ahead. She was so warm and supple, and so apparently available, that his resolve began to weaken. What would it matter if he had his way with her? Or vice versa, as seemed to be the more accurate assessment of the situation. There was no way Chloe could protest. She had, after all, bounced upstairs after that tom like a molly in heat, without giving Rex or anyone else a second glance.

He turned towards Coco. She was very beautiful. Her long, dark hair had such a bright sheen; her skin was so soft and her lips so full. She had a dreamy, demure look on her face, as though she was open to any suggestion he might make, and her hands were wandering all over his body. Her every expression, gesture and movement was sensual and inviting. He put his hand on her thigh and moved his face close to hers, their lips almost touching but not quite. Those peripatetic hands found their way to his crotch, and she gripped with fervour. 'Oh, Rex, you beast,' she whispered. 'Are you going to take me here and now?'

Rex jumped up and stood straight as a ramrod. All the blood rushed from his southern regions up to his face, and he stammered something about going home. Initially flabbergasted but quickly adopting the air of one who knew this would happen and didn't care in the least, Coco unfurled herself from her coiled position on the couch and leaned back. 'You idiot,' she sneered. 'She really has you on a leash, doesn't she?'

'It's not that; it's just that I…'

'Go home, Rex,' she said as she got up and stalked towards her room. 'Take an Uber; we'll need the van in the morning.' And then she was gone. He let himself out.

As he rode the lift down, Rex shook his head and silently berated himself. I am an idiot, he agreed. Chloe didn't even know I existed once that bastard got off the plane. Before, even.

He couldn't know that, upstairs, Chloe was lying awake in that tangle of sheets and fluids, disappointed. Her reunion with Casper had begun well enough in the limo, with him praising her to the skies for the work she was doing and telling her the success of the Australian operation was due to her diligence, catlike charm and wonderful grasp of Felinism.

She had practically purred, and he had stroked her ego, along with her bare inner thigh, all the way from the airport to the hotel. They had raced upstairs to indulge in the mandatory reunification coupling, and at first it went well. But he seemed distant and disinterested at times, and had once called her Sadie. He'd also broken off in the middle of the second act to take a phone call. The caller had been his accountant, and the contents of the call had made him so cross that when he returned to the bed he didn't even pick up where he left off. He licked the back of his left wrist and rubbed it behind his ear, which irritated the shit out of her, and then curled up and closed his eyes. Since then, she'd been staring at the ceiling wondering where Rex was and what he was doing. She rolled over and tried to sleep.

17. Who doesn't love cats?

It can't be what they do for you, which is usually nothing, so it stands to reason that you must love cats for who they are. Sheer force of personality, effortless beauty and endearing aloofness make cats more lovable than even the most self-demeaning dog. Be like a cat.

Casper

Sleep eluded Rex for most of the night. He spent the long, wakeful hours remonstrating with himself for not being man enough to jump Coco's bones, for his painful and ostensibly pointless attachment to Chloe, and for not having the good sense to put a glass of water beside the bed. This last failing forced him to spend an inordinate amount of time trying, without success, to muster up a mouthful of saliva and at least moisten the load of sawdust and gravel that appeared to have taken up residence in his mouth. At last, hours after he'd flopped onto his musty sheets, he dropped off. And seconds later, his phone rang. He knew without looking who it would be, so he leapt for it.

'Hey, Rex.' Chloe sounded cool, and there was just enough of a lack of energy in her voice to make his heart leap. She sounded a bit down, maybe even a bit disheartened, and that was precisely the sort of circumstance he could respond to with boundless love. He hoped that delivering her a great big bouquet of Rex devotion would bring the smile back to her tone. His inner shame for not following through with Coco was already dissipating, replaced with a sense of relief that Chloe hadn't happened upon him in the girls' suite that morning.

'Casper asked me to give you a call,' she began, as Rex experienced the now customary slight deflation. 'There's likely to be a big crowd at the Cat Life Centre today, and he'd – we'd – like you to be our security man. Can you do that?'

'Of course. Love to.' Anything to be near her.

'We also need someone to drive the van over there. Can you get an Uber across here in the next thirty minutes?'

He probably needed a shower, but figured an APC (armpit and crotch) rinse would suffice. He hoped there was enough Rexona in the can to cover any residual BO. 'No problemo.'

As soon as she hung up, he punched in an Uber request, pulled on his rumpled jeans after a quick sniff, and headed to the bathroom to freshen up. Five minutes later, without even treating himself to a cup of coffee, he was out waiting for Omar, his Uber driver. He was feeling much better about his lacklustre response to Coco's overtures and looking forward to assuaging Chloe's unhappiness with his own effervescence.

His happiness was to increase at the hotel. The valet brought the van around, the limousine turned up, and Rex rang upstairs to let Chloe know everything was ready to go. Casper and his little harem came down in one lift, strutting through the lobby looking like a squadron of angels: the girls all in flowing, sinuous white pantsuits, and Casper in a crisp white linen suit with a very pale pink shirt, open to three buttons. The pants were flared and the shoes were as white as the linen. His face was tanned and beautiful, his eyes blazing blue. Everyone in the place turned to look at the glamorous group.

Rex was already in the driver's seat of the van, half excited to see Chloe and half cringing. He expected that she would ride with the boss in the limo, and that when Coco, Yuki and Paris got in with him, they would be laughing at him for failing to grab the opportunity Coco had given him last night. One thing he was certain of – that Coco had already told the others of his pathetic demurral. With luck, Chloe would be in on the gossip, and may even be pleased about it as a sign of his steadfast loyalty to her. As far as the others were concerned, though, he figured the best he could hope for was mocking looks rather than outright derisive laughter.

Casper turned out to have a different transport arrangement in mind, probably because he liked to keep his girls guessing. He invited Yuki and Coco to travel with him, and sent Paris and Chloe off to the van. 'Chloe, you can fill Paris in on the details of the centre, and Paris, you can provide details of the PR work you've done so far,' he said with a shrewd smile.

It was obvious that he wanted to arrive with the luscious young pair, and that Paris and Chloe were being relegated. Paris was fine with it – used to it – but Chloe was huffy. She tried to hide it, but Rex knew her too well for that. He spent the drive trying to cheer her up, while Paris worked on social media posts and emailed various journalists. There was no need for them to talk about the centre, or for Paris to 'fill Chloe in' on the PR side: every Cat Life Centre was a version of every other, and Chloe was across all the PR because that had been her job before she'd started the Subiaco centre. She still loved that side of things and was very good at it.

They arrived at the centre ten minutes before opening, to find a crowd of about twenty cat lovers lining up outside to get in. The limousine driver stopped at the front, where Casper and his ornamental girls got out, while Rex drove around the corner so they could go in via the rear entrance as instructed by Chloe. The last they saw of Casper and the girls as they drove into the laneway was a glimpse of them displaying their flawless felinity to the captivated crowd.

Inside, there was a bustle of meetings and greetings as Casper, Paris, Coco and Yuki were introduced to the local team. Casper made a warm, funny speech that even Rex found inspiring – maybe because Casper had taken the time to single out Rex for his contribution to the design and building – and the staff all sighed and wished the blonde leader was theirs to hold and stroke.

On the button of nine, Rex opened the doors to the by now much larger and even more expectant crowd, every one of them anxious to meet Casper thanks to the power of social media. When they filed in through the cat security doors, the great man was reclining on a beanbag, surrounded by adoring cats, all competing for his magical touch. It looked as though he really did have an amazing rapport with the cats, and the heart of every Felinist or cat lover who saw him fluttered at the sight. Only Paris knew it was an effect achieved through the simple expedient of smearing a bit of Whiskas jelly on each hand and putting cat biscuits in his pockets.

Smiling and petting his attentive furry disciples, Casper looked peaceful and pensive, yet in control. After a full minute of ignoring the gathering crowd to shower love on his feline accoutrements, Casper looked up and seemed surprised to see the people gathered around him, almost as though he'd been woken from a beautiful dream.

He stood up, making even the ungainly act of getting out of a beanbag appear elegant, surreptitiously wiped his hands on a pure silk handkerchief, and greeted the crowd. For the next hour or so he pressed the flesh, spoke with warmth, gentleness and aching sincerity about how much cats meant to him, how fundamental they are to our society, and how wonderful it was to see so many budding Felinists ready to join his modest group. It was touching and uplifting, and the greatest sales tool the Cat Life Centre could ever have.

By 9.45am, journalists and film crews had begun to gather. They were greeted by Paris and Chloe and provided with a press pack containing fact sheets, DVDs, photos of Casper with various cats, and a pure silver key ring in the shape of Bastet sitting regally on an enamel Cat Life Centre logo. On the back were the words, 'Cats were born to rule. Be like a cat.'

As the last of the journalists arrived and took in the splendour of the scene, Casper sashayed around the room, treating both journalists and ordinary cat lovers with equally attentive affection and deference. Chloe and her staff furnished cups of tea and coffee, slices of cake and warm smiles, and rustled up cats for the guests to hold and caress, ensuring that everyone was content.

Over by the door, Rex surveyed the room he'd built with an air of proprietorial diligence, watching how effortlessly Casper charmed and disarmed the attendees. The Cat Man had comprehensively won over every guest, staff member and visiting journalist, and most were following him with their eyes wherever he went, wishing they were the object of his attention. Well, not every one, Rex noted as he locked his vision onto a small, round and rancorous looking customer in the corner, who was staring at Chloe.

18. Dogs love sniffing things out

Cats have the good sense to get bored and move on. Dogs find an interesting scent and follow it to its source, and they don't give up. They gnaw and worry and stick at everything with deplorable, dogged determination, and that makes them annoying. Be like a cat.

Casper

Butch McNab was a journalist, and a pudgy-faced, stocky little bastard. His chest – well, from his shoulders to his hips – was a perfect square sitting on a couple of stout, bowed legs. His head was a ripe, round melon and his face seemed projected flat onto it, the only relief being a short, upturned snout over sneering lips that often bared sharp yellow teeth.

A former cop with a pugnacious insistence on rectitude and integrity in others, Butch had a nose for deceit and corruption, and an itch to right wrongs, whatever it took. He'd hated Casper from the moment he'd heard his name and the caper it was connected to. Cats! He despised cats and everything to do with them, and they loathed and feared him.

'Nasty, smelly man,' seemed to be the typical response of the occasional unwary feline that found itself in his wide circle of personal space, just before it turned tail and ran off. Butch was appalled to be in this place called a Cat Life Centre, surrounded by people fawning over furballs that clearly didn't give a fuck about them. But he had to follow the quarry, and that was the biggest pussy of them all, Casper White.

Eyeballing the golden-haired freak, Butch saw everything he detested in humans and cats alike: that cool, remote confidence, that heavy-lidded stare that says, 'I have secrets but I'll never tell,' and that sleek, easy sexiness that had eluded Butch all his mangy life.

Sneering reflexively, he overcame his desire to rush over and smash that pretty boy right in his smug face. *You don't fool me. I'll get you soon enough, you mongrel*, he thought to himself.

It was true that he already had a couple of good leads. He had friends – police friends – in Los Angeles, and they had introduced him to the San Diego PD, which had been kind enough to keep him in the loop regarding their investigations. While they had been unable to uncover any overt criminal activity – which annoyed them because Casper's cult had some spectacular assets they would have been keen to seize – the IRS's interest had come to light. Butch would be informed of further developments and would reciprocate by keeping the SDPD apprised of his own inquiries. He hoped to find some financial irregularities in the Australian operation, and would also alert the ATO if and when that happened. After he had written the story, of course.

He eyed Chloe, the saucy minx who was running the local show. She was very slinky, and looking seriously self-satisfied at the buzz this inane event was generating, and he hoped to wipe that smug smile off her face sooner rather than later. His lip curled again, and he abruptly felt the odd burning sensation of someone else's gaze boring figurative holes into him. He swivelled his head around until he found the source – the big, dark eyes of Rex watching him watch Chloe, with unnerving intensity. *Hmm, could have trouble with that brute if I'm not careful*, Butch thought. He grinned broadly at Rex and gave a half nod as if to acknowledge a fellow outsider. Rex responded by intensifying his stare, but then looked away in sudden discomfort at the nod. It was almost as if Butch had seen into his soul. He sought out Casper in the crowd and fixed his dark gaze back on the chief enemy. Butch did the same. *This*, he told himself, *could end up being a very interesting case.*

19. Cats are devious

You can never take a cat at face value, because whatever the cat appears to be doing or thinking, there's always an agenda that you don't know about – a deeper plan you're not allowed to share. This is a sign of enormous intelligence and insight, and when you can operate on several levels in the way a cat does, you will be one of the smartest humans alive. Be like a cat.

Casper

At 10.10am, an unhurried ten minutes after the appointed hour for the press conference, by which time some of the journalists had begun to mutter about deadlines and other commitments, Chloe called for attention.

Casper was standing with a small group, holding a wiry little tabby with a white chest, belly and legs, a regal nose and upright bat ears, and a serene, proprietorial expression. It was as though he was her personal property, a gift whose sole purpose was to carry her around, and she knew it.

Everyone in the room snapped to attention at Chloe's command, watching the beautiful young man to see what he would do next. Casper beamed and stroked the cat.

'Look at Cookie,' he said with fatherly pride. 'She's strong, independent, beautiful and comfortable. Wouldn't it be great if we were all like that?'

With infinite care and tenderness, and a look that said nothing was more important to him than the comfort of this cat, Casper put Cookie down on a beanbag, then watched for a few seconds as she prodded and circled, to ensure she would settle in. Hearts fluttered all over the room.

Looking up as Cookie snuggled in and closed her eyes, Casper said, 'Welcome, one and all, to Australia's first Cat Life Centre. Cats have so much to teach us. They're smart, careful, clean, unstressed, focused, fearless, wonderful companions – and they get rid of rats!' He paused for the ripple of laughter to subside.

'Seriously,' he continued, 'cats are more important, more central to our past and our future, than most of you know.' Here he glanced at Chloe, Coco, Paris and Yuki, who had all been initiated into the deeper mysteries of Felinism and were thus the exception, and on cue they all nodded and smiled as only those in possession of knowledge denied others in their presence can.

'And that's why we're here today. From the beginning, it has always been my aim, because it's so important, to bring my discovery about cats home to Australia. And make no mistake: what I have revealed is momentous – a historic and life-changing discovery. Thousands – hundreds of thousands – of happy people in the United States have already shared the secrets of Felinism, and for every one of them it has brought something special, something wonderful into their lives. Now it's Australia's turn. Thanks to the spectacular efforts of the gorgeous Chloe, her talented and dedicated builder, Rex, and their team, the Subiaco Cat Life Centre is a reality.

'I love this place. It's filled with life and laughter, comfort and warmth, and best of all, beautiful, approachable and responsive cats who are here for no other purpose than to help us learn how to be more like them. They're teaching us how to love, how to live, how to deal with each other, and how to find the serenity they carry within themselves. It's just amazing. This is to be the first of many, many Cat Life Centres around the country. I intend to bring the wonders of Felinism to every corner of my homeland, and I promise to visit every one of my Cat Life Centres.'

There followed the familiar sales patter around Felinism, the role of cats, the marvellous time visitors could have interacting with or simply admiring the resident felines, exhortations to delve into the enlightening philosophies of Felinism, and so on. For many, it was a new idea, and more than a few found it inspiring. Casper gave off such a positive vibe, the entire Felinism tribe was so dazzling, and the endless antics of the cats, whether on the screens or cavorting around the room in the furry flesh, were so engaging that the attendees were all – with one or two notable exceptions – smitten.

At last, the spiel was over, and Casper graciously allowed that he would answer a few questions. The floor erupted, with the army of slim blonde television reporters leading the charge. 'How many cats do you have, Mr White?' 'Is it true you can actually speak to cats?' 'Where will the next Cat Life Centre be opening, and when?' 'What's the secret of your meteoric success?' 'Do you think you'll have the same impact on the lives of Australians as you've had in the United States?'

Every time Butch McNab tried to ask his question – is it true you left the United States because you're under investigation, Mr White? – he was drowned out by the chorus of adoring Dorothy Dixes, every one of whom would later deliver glowing television, radio, press and online reports on this welcome addition to the growing panoply of pseudo-religious obsessions vying for their slice of the zeitgeist.

Eventually Butch slunk out, shaking his head. He realised that he was fighting a losing battle, but was not yet ready to concede the war. He would catch the Cat Man at another time and place.

Chloe at last waded into the fray, declaring the event over and suggesting that Mr White had many more significant matters to attend to. As the media made for the exits and the plebeian guests settled into cat heaven and coffee, Casper gave Chloe a big hug and whispered something in her ear that made her nipples, barely concealed beneath her clingy outfit, harden.

Rex witnessed this and was dismayed. He turned away, ashamed of his negative reaction, so he didn't see that as Casper moved away, Chloe turned to regard him – Rex – with astonishment, and perhaps a hint of jealousy.

20. Cats and dogs need each other

Cats are superior to dogs in every way. They're smarter, cleaner, much less prone to excess, and nowhere near as easily distracted. But that doesn't mean there is no place for dogs in the world. Dogs, it must be admitted, have qualities that cats don't share, and in certain situations they are very useful. Cats need dogs, and so do people. But never let them forget who is in charge.

Casper

In truth, there were not any other matters Casper needed to attend to, significant or otherwise. There was, however, an image to maintain. So Paris spoke to Casper in exaggeratedly businesslike tones, holding a thick diary open before her, as the bedazzled media dragged themselves out of the Cat Life Centre to go back to their offices and studios to compose and record enthralled reports.

Casper dallied with the cats and customers for a while, endearing himself to felines and humans alike with his casual splendour and easy manner, but eventually Paris managed to drag him towards the rear exit. Rex assumed it was time for his nap.

The plan had been for Rex to take Coco and Yuki back to the hotel, stopping wherever they wanted to on the way, while Paris and Casper returned to the hotel together in the limo to plan their next PR assault. Chloe was to stay at the Cat Life Centre to manage the buzzing crowd and bubbling staff, and would catch up with the rest for dinner.

But there had been a change of plans, Chloe tersely informed Rex while Casper was in conference with a kitten. Rex was to accompany Casper in the limo and, as the only other holder of an Australian driver's licence, she was to drive the other three back to the hotel.

Rex had never been in a proper limousine before, and he was excited at the prospect. He and his cricket team had once hired a stretch Hummer after winning their local championship, but Rex had already necked quite a few beers by the time they'd been picked up, and all he remembered was pressing, perspiring bodies, thumping music and pulsing purple lights. On reflection, it had been more of a crowded, kitsch, all-male disco on wheels than a limo ride.

So he was looking forward to this new experience. He was even enthusiastic about sharing with the boss, because in spite of the Cat Man's attentions to Chloe, and her manifest physical reaction, he'd been impressed by Casper's talk and by the way he handled the adulation heaped on him. He couldn't deny it: he was fascinated by Casper and wanted to get to know him.

'Casper wants to talk to you,' Chloe hissed while he was musing on the magic of limousine travel and the possibility of bonding with the Cat Man. 'What have you done?'

'Nothing.' At least as far as he knew. But the seed had been sown; maybe this wasn't to be the joyride he'd envisioned. Maybe Casper was going to pay out on him for knocking back

Coco. Perhaps he would after all find fault with the construction of the Cat Life Centre. Then another, ugly thought struck him, and with an inward groan, he hoped that the purpose of the trip was not for the bastard to crow about what a great root Chloe was. Though maybe that wouldn't be such a bad thing, because he could at least flash a knowing smile and say, 'Yeah, I know.' Whatever it was about, he hoped it wouldn't end in them getting in a fight. Chloe would never talk to him again if he was forced to beat the living shit out of Mr Alpha.

The man himself sauntered over with a wide, assumed – Rex presumed – smile. The kind of smile that a crocodile might have on its dial just before it snaps its jaws across the victim's torso.

'Rex!' he said with an outbreak of effusiveness. 'I need to have a quiet word with you, mate. Join me in the limo back to the pub?' Rex hated that this handsome devil, with so much else going for him, also spoke his own language. And so well at that. Damn, he was charming. How could such a short relationship as theirs already be so replete with competing emotions?

'Sure,' was all he said.

'Vehicle's waiting; let's go. Just don't forget to give the van keys to Chloe.' So fucking affable, and thoughtful too.

Handing over the keys as ordered, even Rex – as dim and colour-blind as his perception often seemed to be – could see that Chloe was quietly seething. He searched in vain for ear steam. He still had no idea of what he had done to upset her.

With a rock-star wave at the assembled cat lovers and cultists, the dashing guru ushered Rex out of the building and into the plush confines of the car. The disappointingly plush confines of the car, as far as Rex was concerned. He hadn't known what to expect, but he thought the limo would be bigger, richer, ritzier or at least more exclusive looking.

Instead, it smelled like upholstery and stale celebrity sweat, and the carpet was dotted with sticky, expensive spillages and cigar burns. There's nothing more disheartening, Rex found, than learning that the rich and famous are as clumsy and malodorous as the rest of us, and travel in vehicles that are really just cars, only bigger. That gaudy Hummer disco was starting to look good.

Casper was very relaxed, and took to cleaning his ears with the licked back of his wrists. Rex didn't know whether to snot him or give him a big bear hug. How could something so annoying be so adorable? He stared out the window and watched the green lushness of Kings Park roll by, desperate to wind down the window and put his head out in the fresh air. He could almost smell the lemon-scented gums and the peppery redolence of the shaggy she-oaks whizzing past.

After a while, Casper fixed a cool, benign eye on his fellow passenger, who responded by trying not to squirm.

'You did a great job on the Cat Life Centre, mate,' he began. He seemed genuine, but then, he always did. Rex wondered if he would ever master the art of faking sincerity as well as Casper did.

'Chloe told me how hard you worked, how smart your designs were and how your clever craftsmanship made all the difference to the centre. You should be congratulated.'

Rex mumbled thanks and tried to disappear into himself. He didn't take compliments well, probably because most often a compliment was followed by a dismissal, an insult or an onerous request. He wondered which would be forthcoming.

'So far, you've proven yourself a great asset to Felinism,' said Casper, to Rex's surprise and consternation. A double compliment undoubtedly presaged a proper mauling. 'I think you'd be a very valuable permanent member of our team, and I'd like to initiate you into the miracles of Felinism myself. I'd also like you to come with me on the national tour, as my personal security officer. What do you say?'

The offer to go next-level with the cult threw Rex. He didn't mind the whole cat thing, and it was after all a great conversation starter, but did he want to become a full-on disciple? He wasn't sure. The idea of travelling as Casper's bodyguard had obvious upsides, but there were clear down-sides too. Rather than give an immediate answer, he decided to test Casper's commitment.

'Chloe says I'm a dog,' he said.

'So you are,' said Casper with a smile. 'You're a true dog, and you may never be a genuine cat. But that doesn't mean you can't travel with us, learn more about us and try to be more like us. In any case, it's nothing to be ashamed of. I put shit on dogs all the time, because that's what cats do.' He smiled again, with heart-stirring honesty. 'But the fact of the matter is, the world needs dogs. Shit, cats need dogs more than anyone else does. You're the *yang* to our *yin*, the foil to our swords, the strop to our razor. But more than that, dogs have qualities we need. You're smart; you're loyal, devoted and strong.

'Do you think I would leave everything to cats? No way. Things would be left undone or half done, like a half-eaten pigeon or a poorly covered turd, and little things like honesty, diligence and vigour would be in too short a supply. So I like to keep a few dogs around me, to get things done and to keep my cats on their toes.

'My financial controller back in San Diego, she's a Dobermann. My head of security in the US is a Rottweiler. Our logistics guy is like a beautifully trained sheepdog. And you; you, my friend, are a big, shaggy, powerful German shepherd. You're friendly, intelligent and easy to get along with, but you can also be fierce and a little bit scary, and when shit gets serious, you're the man I want to have by my side. You're not just a dog, mate, you're a man, and a good one.'

Damn. This bloke just kept on coming up with surprises. Rex felt flattered, and he had a new respect for Casper's perspicacity in seeing his true self and worth so clearly. No one had ever called him intelligent before, but suddenly he felt he was just that. The idea of being a security chief in a smart black suit, with an earpiece and wrap-around sunglasses, and maybe even a concealed weapon or two, appealed to his ego and sense of adventure. He could always go back to being a chippy if it didn't work out. But it would, his inner voice insisted. He'd swan around the country – maybe the world – at Casper's side, using his sheer menace to scare off any would-be attackers or malcontents. It would be a fuckin' lark. And he'd soon forget about Chloe, because he'd have his hands full wrangling the bevy of beautiful young women that flocked around the boss, occasionally pairing off with his pick of the many who didn't make the alpha tom's grade.

Casper could see Rex's eyes shining and almost hear his mind ticking over, and he knew he'd won his man. 'What do you reckon, Rexy?' he said. He held out his hand in an almost-submissive gesture. Rex seized it in his big, hairy paw and shook it with enthusiasm.

'You're on,' he said.

Casper tried not to look too much like he'd just eaten the whole canary in one bite, but it didn't matter because Rex wasn't paying that much attention – his mind was already 'on tour.'

'Excellent. You work for me now.'

21. Cats didn't evolve – they arrived

Cats are our rightful masters; there is no doubt about that. They came here and they created us. And when the time comes for cats to go home, we Felinists will go with them. The rest of humanity ... well, let's just say they'll wish they'd been more like cats.

Casper

The rest of the ride was quiet, as both men were wrapped in their own thoughts and plans. Getting out at the hotel, the two parted as friends. Casper retired to his suite for a catnap, and Rex sat in the lobby for a few minutes collecting his thoughts. He wasn't sure he wanted to become a top-level Felinist, but if he wanted to become a cool, menacing security hunk, flitting around fending off fans and foes for Casper, he'd have to go through with it.

What with all the travel, the suit-buying and the looking good, and surrounded as he would be by Casper's adoring devotees and in the prime position to catch his cast-offs, he'd be sure to forget about Chloe. Then again, becoming a Level Three initiate might bring him closer to Chloe. Perhaps she'd find a new respect for him once he'd been admitted to the upper echelon, and who knew what might happen then?

He was aware that in the space of a few seconds he'd considered becoming a fully-fledged Felinist as a way of both distancing himself from Chloe and getting closer to her, but he didn't see that as a direct contradiction. Either outcome would be acceptable.

While he was musing thus, Yuki and Coco came bounding in, full of pretty, kittenish enthusiasm, followed somewhat more sedately by Chloe and Paris, the latter pair talking PR opportunities and social media strategies.

Chloe seemed to have moved past her earlier mood, giving Rex a bright smile.

'Sooo, Rexy,' she purred. 'What did you two naughty boys talk about? Not me, I hope?' Missing the compliment bait she had so obviously cast, Rex shook his shaggy head.

'Oh, no,' he said. 'Casper wants me to go on tour with him. He's going to induct me into the top level.'

Chloe allowed neither her disbelief at this turn of events nor her disappointment that her name hadn't dominated their discussion to blight her frozen smile.

'Wow,' she said with contrived gaiety. 'How exciting! Casper must think very highly of you. You're a lucky boy.'

A more perceptive person might have noticed the narrowing of the eyes and the tight frostiness of the smile, but Rex took her words at face value and grinned like a clown.

'Oh, yeah,' he said. 'This is going to be awesome.'

At that moment, Coco and Yuki, who'd been dallying by the gift shop, descended on Rex like a cloud of perfume and chiffon. 'Take us back to Fremantle for a seafood lunch, Rexy?'

He agreed with alacrity, hoping that the embarrassment brought on by his refusal of Coco's advances could be overcome by a fun afternoon together. Chloe dropped the van keys into his hand with a significant look.

'You can drop me back at work on the way through,' she said. The way she leaned on the word *work*, as though it was a solid steel bar that could support the combined weight of all of them, was something even Rex couldn't miss. But he was confused. What had he done wrong? He thought she'd have been happy for him. He shrugged and said, 'Let's go.'

They all piled into the van and, following the detour to drop a taciturn Chloe off at the Cat Life Centre, struck out for Fremantle via the coast. The girls fell in love with the clear water and white sand of Cottesloe Beach, and after dipping their toes in the cool Indian Ocean, insisted on lunching in the tearooms overlooking the tranquil blue bay, which was teeming with sun worshippers and tiny, stinging jellyfish. The meal was expensive but delicious, and the servings large enough for a hungry lion. He was glad he wasn't paying.

Sated and hungry for action, the trio pressed on to Fremantle, where they toured the Round House. A powerful circular prison perched on a headland overlooking Bathers Beach just south of Fremantle Harbour, it had been built by the prisoners it was to encase almost two hundred years before. When it was done, the builders were incarcerated there in cruel, overcrowded conditions, and it had become an abyss of torture, sickness and violence. By the time the three pleasure-seekers happened upon it, the Round House had long since been cleaned, sanitised and commercialised, and the girls were enchanted.

They strolled around the streets of the port's beautifully preserved West End in the warm autumn sunshine, marvelling at the colonial architecture and dozy afternoon quiet, at last walking through a whalers' tunnel dug into the solid limestone beneath the Round House, to repair to a bar on Bathers Beach. As the sun sank, they indulged and talked story and laughed and forgot the past, and Rex felt that he had achieved his objective of leaving any awkwardness between them behind.

He dropped the girls off tipsy and giggling. There was no repeat invitation upstairs, which came as a relief, so he drove the van home. He figured he was doing Casper a solid by not making him pay the extortionate valet parking fees.

The next morning, Rex went up to Casper's suite. They were to spend the better part of the day in conclave, the master schooling his pupil on the inner mysteries of Felinism.

Rex found himself nervous, wondering what he was about to embark on, as he knocked on the door. It was one of those days that come with the sense that whatever happened, his life was about to change. But then again, there had been quite a few of those lately, so he should be getting used to the feeling. He swallowed the lump of misgivings – or was that toast and vegemite? – in his throat, ready to press on regardless because … well, because Chloe. Good or bad, the outcome would involve her, and that was all the inducement he needed.

The door swung open fast and wide, and there was Casper in yet another crisp white outfit, looking fresh, ready and welcoming. He didn't just shake Rex's hand; he drew him into a big hug that he held for just long enough to make it a tiny bit weird, then pushed Rex into the room. Rex was disoriented and dizzied by this unexpected reception, so he stood looking like a big, dumb animal as Casper closed the door and locked it, swished past him a fraction too close for comfort, and threw himself on the couch. To Rex's immense relief – he was sure the Cat Man would make him sit next to him – Casper pointed at the seat opposite. 'Sit,' he said, and Rex obeyed like the good dog-boy he was.

Casper poured them each a coffee from a pot already placed on the table, offered Rex a biscuit – which he declined because his throat was suddenly dry – and sat back looking relaxed.

'Well, here we are, big guy,' said the Cat Man with a genial smile. Rex nodded, unsure of how he was supposed to reply. 'You are about to become a Level Three Felinist and one of my most trusted lieutenants. But don't let that thought pressure you,' Casper said, piling on the pressure. 'Just relax, take it all in and save your questions for later. We'll start with what you already know.'

He began with the Level Two story of the cats' enlightenment of humans across the Fertile Crescent, originating in the area between the Tigris and Euphrates rivers and stretching across to the Nile and the worship of Bastet and Mafdet. He explained that cats had implanted the ideas that led to the development of agriculture, architecture, mathematics and science in the minds of the humans living at the dawn of what we now call civilisation, and encouraged them to enhance their mental capacity further by exploring those disciplines.

This outline was, as Casper had acknowledged, not new to Rex. He'd already been confirmed as a Level Two Felinist, and returned part of his salary to the organisation as required. In this elongated and elaborated version, Casper furnished a lot of details that Chloe had skipped through, and it took quite a long time. It was interesting, but it was also densely packed with tiring minutiae, so Rex nodded a lot, helped himself to the sandwiches and snacks Casper had provided, and tried to stay focused. Or at least to look as though he was.

By lunchtime, in spite of the tedium, he was convinced that Casper was actually onto something. The guru's masterful telling of the tale was partly responsible for its power to convince, but the blunt force that is repetition, the favoured tool of propagandists, was also at work. Rex had heard the story enough times to make it familiar, and every time he heard it again, it crept a little further into his brainbox and nestled a little deeper.

Following a lavish room-service lunch, Casper opened the wide double doors and invited Rex onto the wide balcony for the afternoon's lesson. With the silvery expanses of the Swan River glittering before them, and the cluster of Perth's skyscrapers shining bright in the afternoon sun as a backdrop, Casper laid out the deeper truth of Felinism: the secrets of Level Three.

'This is sacred information,' he began. 'You must solemnly swear never, ever to divulge even the tiniest iota of what I am about to tell you. On your life.'

'Sure,' said Rex, still picking at the chips that had come with his burger.

'Say it. Say, "I swear on my life," ' insisted Casper. He was in unconditional earnest.

'I swear on my life,' said Rex, holding up his right hand as though he was a cyclist indicating a stop.

'If you do, if you ever spill so much as a word of this, I will track you down and kill you. And you know I'm a hunter.'

Rex had not, in the short time since they had met, spent a lot of time staring into Casper's eyes. But he did so as the cult leader pronounced this last sentence, and he saw cold steel in their chill blue depths. There was murder behind them.

'Okay,' said Rex. He had no idea what else to say. Internally, he was repressing the nagging question of how and why he was being drawn into this thing.

'Okay,' Casper repeated back to him. 'What I am about to tell you is one hundred percent true. I can't tell you how I know it, or how I know it is both accurate and factual, but I assure you that it is, and that you will see the truth of it fully revealed in your lifetime. You will be one of the lucky ones, thanks to what I'm about to tell you, and thanks to me.' He smiled in a benevolent, self-satisfied way. 'You owe me, Rex. Don't let me down.'

'I swear I won't, Casper,' said Rex, with as much confidence as a man with a rapidly retreating grasp on reality could muster.

'Okay, to recap. You're a Level Two Felinist, so you know all about cats and the ancient people, and how this dumb ape that had been lumbering around the planet for, like, millions of years, suddenly got smart, practically overnight. We started building stuff and discovering all sorts of fundamental physical and philosophical truths that accelerated our journey from being dim wanderers to the masters of the planet. Most curious of all, we started doing things that, by the greatest of coincidences, made life easier, more comfortable and more fun for cats. We built grain silos that attracted their favourite prey; we created comfy, cosy homes and we invited cats into them. In fact, we made them feel like honoured guests, as we still do, giving them fluffy cushions to sleep on and special toilets that we empty for them. And we feed them two or more times a day. Remarkable, no?'

'Um, yeah, I guess.' Rex had had this stuff on high rotation in the months he'd been working on and for the Cat Life Centre, so it was ingrained.

'Now, I have a question for you, Rex.' Casper's eyes were burning into his; the bloke's passion, at least, could not be denied. 'Where were all the cats before they turned up, unannounced, eight or more centuries ago?'

'Huh?'

'The cats. *Felis catus* – the common domestic cat. Unknown until they were allegedly domesticated by the ancient Mesopotamians, then turning up one day as instant objects of reverence and worship in ancient Egypt, on the other end of the Fertile Crescent. Where were they before then?'

'I dunno. Evolving, I s'pose.'

'Wrong. Before they showed up mysteriously as full-blown gods, cats were nowhere to be seen. All their supposed ancestors, the so-called felids, are fucking monsters. Lions, cheetahs, cougars, sabre-toothed tigers and such. And out of nowhere comes the small, short-haired domestic cat. It seems odd because it is.'

Rex thought of all the other, smaller kinds of felids – lynxes, civets, bobcats and so on, but he couldn't be sure if there had been any of them in North Africa eight or so thousand years ago, so he kept his mouth shut. Probably a prudent move, because to contradict Casper at this point, or even to interrupt his passionate dissertation, could prove damaging to his prospects in the organisation, if not his health.

'You may have noticed,' Casper said, changing tack, 'that cats aren't very dexterous. Unlike you, my friend, cats are no good with their hands.' Here, he grabbed Rex's big, gnarled hands for effect, and turned them over to inspect his calloused palms. 'Look at these things. Perfect for building, creating, carrying, fixing. Also for stroking, petting and patting,' he added with a sly grin. 'Your average cat, she doesn't have hands, she has paws. Useless for almost anything other than holding a rat's body nice and tight while she removes its head, or tearing out a dove's intestines.'

He dropped Rex's hands, and with an extended index finger tapped his temple. 'But cats don't need hands, and they only use their paws for pleasure, because they have their minds. And it's always been that way. They can project their thoughts, their wishes and their ideas, and get other, more nimble-limbed creatures to do their bidding for them. They mastered physics and chemistry and mathematics and architecture and a hundred other things thousands, maybe millions of years ago, using nothing but their brains. Think of how mind-bogglingly smart they must be! Do you know of any other creature on this planet with such powerful mind-projection abilities as the common house cat? Of course not.

'Cats are unlike any other animal on earth because they're not from earth. Because cats – as we know them – didn't evolve. They arrived. They came from the planet Meon, at precisely the right historical juncture for humans, on a mission.'

Casper ignored the alarmed look on Rex's face at this revelation; he'd seen it many, many times before.

'Cats evolved on the planet Meon, and rather than change their own physical form through evolution, they stayed the same and put other creatures to work for them to realise their ideas and plans. But they've never, in all their millennia as mental giants, been able to find the ultimate vehicles for putting their thoughts into action. The beasts they co-opted on their home planet served a purpose, in that they built the homes, the devices, the computers and other things the cats needed, including interstellar rocket ships. But the smart ones always rebelled, and the dumb ones couldn't always get it right.

'Even under these trying circumstances, cats made some amazing advances – way, way more than we can even imagine. But they've never found the perfect manual labourer. The ideal worker. They're an indomitable species, though, and they set out across the galaxy to find the right mix of brains and physical capability. That's how they came to land here – literally land here – eight or ten thousand years ago. To see if earth might be home to a creature that could be moulded into their ideal labourer.'

'Slave,' said Rex. He didn't mean to, but the word just popped out of his mouth.

'Well, yeah,' admitted Casper. 'But being a slave to cats is still being the one to carry out the bidding of the gods. It's an honour. A blessing.'

'Okay,' said Rex, trying hard to believe. It did seem logical that cats, who could well have amazing brains but would always be woefully bad with their hands – or paws, as the case may be – would need someone or something to do all the tricky manual stuff for them. Further, it was indeed a curious coincidence that human intellectual development had taken such a giant leap forward, after thousands upon thousands of years of mentally treading water, at exactly the same time that cats appeared on earth.

Casper's explanation had a compelling ring of truth to it, and even if it was a complete fabrication, at least it was an alluring story. And surely something that far-fetched couldn't be completely untrue, could it? It sounded at once so fantastic and so plausible that there must be a grain or two of truth in it.

'So, the cat explorers landed here, under the command of a cat named Freyja, and found these wonderful man-apes with large, malleable brains and two marvellous flexible, adaptable appendages, with five strong, fine digits attached to each.' He was holding Rex's hands again. 'These are accessories that can work at large or small scale, and are exquisitely set up to wield all sorts of tools that can magnify or microfy the scale of their work.' Rex was pondering the existence, or otherwise, of the word 'microfy', and wondering why, if it existed, people ever bothered to use the much longer 'miniaturise'. Casper continued, oblivious to Rex's etymological musings.

'The owners of these marvellous members, the people they found living on the planet, weren't what we would call advanced when the cats arrived. They'd developed a range of simple implements, but their communication systems were limited if they existed at all, and their cultures were even more rudimentary. Anything they learned or thought of had to be passed down from one generation to the next orally, with all the inherent unreliability of that method, or lost entirely. The following generations often had to acquire all over again the lessons their antecedents had learned but forgotten to pass down, or had distorted and corrupted in the telling.

'The cats could see that although the humans' ambitions and accomplishments were basic, their hardware was good. They just needed to have their software upgraded. And that is the cats' specialty.

'They gave a small group of people over by the fertile lands between the Tigris and Euphrates rivers a bit of an imaginationary kick-start. Using the telepathic skills we have all seen cats display countless times, but which were infinitely more potent back then, they slowly fed those *Homo sapiens* ideas and began building their mental capacities. It started with the simple stuff – the first cab off the rank being the idea of planting and tending crops in one place rather than chasing food all over the countryside as they had been doing for millions of years. They followed with concepts for permanent structures to live in, to store grain and other things in. Then, much later, as things began to gather pace, they implanted more advanced thoughts in their human subjects' minds – numeracy, written records and more detailed, nuanced language.

'The elastic, expandable human brain responded by taking those ideas and running with them. Once the experiment, designed by the supreme leader of the cats on Meon, was underway, most of the cats got back on their spaceship, leaving a number of their kind behind as caretakers and trial monitors, and continued on their quest. At last count, cats had seeded over a thousand different species, on almost as many planets, with similar ideas and technological thinking. They give each new breed of cat worker a gestational period in which to develop their skills to full potential – around eight thousand years in our case, due to the vagaries of near-light-speed travel and the dilation of time at that speed – and then return to see whether the subjects have developed to the stage where they are worthy of the definitive reward: transfer back to Meon. They call it the Great Experiment.

'Our part in the Great Experiment is almost over. We've reached the stage where Muit, the supreme leader of the cats, can make a determination as to the suitability or dispensability of human beings as the ones chosen to carry out the cats' grand plan, and they're on their way back. They'll be here soon. And any humans that have an accurate understanding of our true relationship with cats, and who show an appropriate level of veneration for them, will be taken back to their home world along with all terrestrial cats. On arrival, we'll be shown a world of great and astounding creations and ideas, and given a life we could never even dream about.'

Casper's eyes were shining and there was a thin sheen of perspiration on his upper lip. He looked as though he was on the verge of orgasm. There was a confusion of thoughts and reactions milling about in Rex's mind. He couldn't tell if it was the greatest load of tripe he'd ever heard, an inspired allegory for the journey of human development, or an insight into the most important truth ever discovered.

Unable to account for the seeming coincidence of the unheralded arrival of *Felis catus* as a species and the spark of genius that thrust humanity into generations of explosive creativity and discovery, he also could not deny that the ancient people of the Fertile Crescent, who kicked the whole thing off, worshipped cats. So there was a connection, however circumstantial. Above all, he couldn't say the whole thing was any more or less preposterous than some of the other beliefs people around the world held sacred.

But there was one anomaly he couldn't get past. 'If cats are the masters and we are their slaves, why are cats our pets?'

The glint in Casper's eye suggested that he'd been expecting or, to be more accurate, hoping for that question. 'Ah,' he said. 'This is where the Great Experiment, like so many the cats have tried on so many worlds, has had an unforeseen outcome – not disastrous in terms of human advancement or our suitability for the tasks they'll give us on Meon, quite the opposite, but crucial nonetheless. You see, when they upgraded the human software, the upgrade took on a life of its own. It achieved spectacular results, but it also awoke in humans a desire for inquiry and accomplishment, and, later, conquest, domination and war. The cats had unleashed an unstoppable machine, as though they had invented an AI – an artificial intelligence – that took over its own destiny.'

Rex nodded. He knew the term.

'The downside is that the cats that had been left here on earth, as per their brief, sat back and let the experiment run its course. Their input waned, while our propensity for progress took over.

'Over the hundreds and hundreds of generations since then, cats have let their powers lapse to an extent. It's debatable whether this was intentional or accidental, and even if the current generation of cats has any idea of their true power; but it's there within them. And when their fellow felines return to finalise the experiment, it will be reawakened.' He paused. 'You seem sceptical, my friend.'

This was a jolt, but Rex hadn't been as successful as he hoped in keeping the chary, suspicious expression off his face. Casper looked as though he was about to spring a trap, but Rex knew that he had to blunder into it, if only to find out what it was. 'I just can't see that any master – because that's what you're saying cats are, our masters – would allow themselves to lose their power. Who would give it away, or let it slip away like that?'

Chuckling softly, Casper shook his head so that his silky blonde hair shimmered scintillatingly, the way the Swan River was sparkling below them.

'Oh, my boy,' he answered with a knowing smile. 'Who would give their power away? You. Me. Everyone.'

Rex cocked his head and arched one eyebrow.

'The human race, and in fact every species across the universe that has risen to the position of being creators, has the same basic flaw. The things they – we – create to make their lives easier, or richer, or more accomplished in any sense, all, almost without exception, end up turning the tables. The creation becomes the master, the creator the slave.

'You don't believe me, I can see. No matter, it's an easy point to prove. Take us humans. We created money to facilitate trade, and then banks to manage the money. Today, we are captives of both. We work to make money, yes, to buy things but mostly to pay back the money that we borrow from banks – money they create out of thin air. They own the money, they own us, and far from making our lives easier, money and banks rule our every waking moment.

'Not convinced? Let's talk about cars. Motor cars were invented to make getting around easier and faster. So what happened? They took over, and now our cities are designed and built to accommodate them – even if it means inconvenience and danger. Not only that, we continue to deplete and poison the planet to serve the cars we created.

'And how about the television, the newspaper, the radio and that great villain of our times, the internet – the motley collection of ratbag items we call the media? We invented media to share information and ideas with each other, but what happened? The media, directed by an unelected few, have come to control the flow of ideas. At the whim of their owners, the media restrict and suppress our access to some information, and flood us with the "information" they deem it expedient for us to have. The greater the extent of media, the more control an ever-smaller number of people wield.

'I could go on giving you powerful examples – government, educational institutions, pharmaceuticals and more, but I think you get the drift. We create things to give us freedom, and we become the servants of those things. Cats created us in a very real sense, but they didn't allow themselves to become our vassals, although they have over time consented to becoming our pets. We feed them and house them and pamper them, and we never, ever make them work. I think they did very well.'

Eyes wide, throat working as he swallowed this chunk of indigestible but undeniable facts, Rex sat back and stared at Casper. 'Wow, I never thought of it that way.'

'Nobody ever does.'

'You know, you should be out there telling people that. Let them know the truth about the things they think make their lives easier, but that in reality control them.'

'Oh mate,' said Casper. 'I can run around the world saying whatever shit I like about cats, and no one will give a fat rat's arse. But if I start talking about where power truly resides in this world, the people behind it would kill me in a minute.' He laughed – a pure and natural laugh that Rex knew was sincere. This was possibly the most genuine, unmanufactured moment he'd seen or heard from the Cat Man in their acquaintance. He liked Casper then.

He laughed along with the blonde guru and said, 'True.'

'So, anyway, back to Felinism,' said Casper with a serious look. 'The Great Experiment hasn't gone completely as planned, but it did change humans from aimless, uncultured nomads into intelligent, creative and dexterous creatures who would be of great use to the cats on Meon. When they return, the cats will be keen to assess our talents and suitability for the things they need us to do on Meon. Importantly, they will need to assure themselves that if they take any of us home with them, those chosen few will not cause problems. They will know, very soon after arriving, if they don't already, of our accomplishments in the arts of weaponry and killing and war, and they will understand how treacherous and threatening most humans are. By choosing to take us Felinists with them, they can be sure they're getting people who understand our relationship to cats, and will be thrilled to work for and with them. For our part, we'll get to see cats in all their true majesty and be astounded by the might of their minds. Ours will be a match literally made in the heavens.

'While it's a given that they will take Felinists with them, it's more than probable that it will only be Felinists, because the rest of humanity is too unreliable, too lazy in many cases, and too fierce and acquisitive in others. Only the intelligent and enlightened will go with them. And that now means you, Rex.'

'What happens to the other humans that don't go with the cats?' Rex asked the question even though he was already certain of the answer.

'The experiment will be terminated,' said Casper. 'The cats won't be able to afford to have a duplicitous, technologically aware and violent species like ours eventually roaming around the galaxy causing trouble.'

'Oh. I guess not.' The implications were too great to fit into Rex's mind, threatening to cause a tsunami of cognitive dissonance, so he ignored them.

'So, how do you feel?' Casper was bright, expectant, shiny in the afternoon sun. Below, a waterskier was towed onto a ski jump on the Swan River, its waters glittering gold in the light. He soared briefly, then crashed into the water with a splash. The traffic kept whizzing by and the humans of Perth went about their mundanely momentous lives.

'Well, it's a lot to take in,' Rex answered truthfully. 'But if it's true, it's an amazing story, and an incredible opportunity.'

Excitement at the prospect of being one of the chosen few to be whisked away to the cat planet somewhere in a whole new part of the universe, was helping him overcome his misgivings regarding the truth of the tale and the sanity of its teller. The idea that he would travel across the galaxy, would be saved when the rest of the population was put to the sword, and see the glories cats had created on other worlds, was irresistible. It made him feel special.

'Thank you for initiating me, and for trusting me in this, Casper. You can't know how much I appreciate it. I'll try and be a good Felinist. The best I can be. And I'm sure that as I grow to become more like a cat – more like you – I'll understand and believe better.'

The Cat Man rewarded him with a broad, patronising smile. 'I'm sure you will, my boy.' And then he added, 'You know, you're a lot smarter than Chloe gives you credit for.'

'She doesn't give me much credit for anything.' Reminded of her, Rex cast his eyes down and made a grumpy face.

'Well, she will,' said Casper adamantly. 'I don't know why you put so much stock in what she thinks or does anyway. She's just a pussy.' It was a throwaway remark, intended to show solidarity and indicate some sort of brotherhood between them, and Rex understood that. But hearing Chloe denigrated like that, reduced to a stereotype and objectified to such a demeaning extent, made the hackles on his neck rise.

22. Dogs can be guarded

Dogs may be impetuous and at times quite reckless, but there are also occasions when they act out of well-placed prudence. They see what must be done and they do it, even if their instinct is to do otherwise. We see this as evidence that over the millennia, dogs have been studying the behaviour of cats and emulating them. Even dogs try to be more like cats.

Casper

'So jealous.'

'What?'

'What?'

'What's so jealous?'

'Not what, who. Me. I'm so jealous of you right now.'

'Ah.' Rex was none the wiser. They were back at the bar named after a punctuation mark, and Chloe was looking at him with eyes wide enough to swallow him whole, though as the exchange noted above progressed, those eyes had narrowed and the face on which they featured had begun to appear annoyed.

'People don't have to say "I'm so jealous" any more; they

can say, "So jealous" and everyone gets it. It's a thing.'

Rex didn't bother asking what a thing was. He knew it would impede the progress he appeared to have been making.

'Why would you ever be jealous of me?'

'Because you're going on tour with Casper, silly.' Her amusement was honest, as if the source of her jealousy was the plainest thing in the world, like a black spot in the middle of a white cat's face.

'Ah,' he said again. He didn't want to appear any more stupid than he already felt, though the fact that he was mulling over the evident redundancy of the use of personal pronouns was probably an indicator that he wasn't as stupid as he felt.

'You're so lucky to be going with them,' Chloe said. She was glowing with an odd intensity, her eyes almost moist at the thought of Rex heading off into the wild blue yonder with Casper and the girls.

'Think of what you'll see. What you'll learn. Oh, Rexy, you will stay in touch, won't you? Let me know where you are and what he … um, you're doing?'

'Sure, you know I'd love to talk to you every day if I could.' He'd noticed the little slip, but was prepared to overlook it if it meant regular contact with Chloe.

She changed the subject. 'So, how does it feel to be a Level Three Felinist? Isn't it amazing?'

He didn't quite know how to handle that. He was still feeling somewhat ambivalent about the whole thing. On the one hand, the story was so fantastic it couldn't possibly be true. But on the other, it was so improbable that it couldn't be made up. He vacillated between trusting Casper and wanting to be with him all the time, hating him because of the hold he had over Chloe, and thinking of him as a con man. But whenever he thought about it, he couldn't deny that he felt special. Casper had chosen him, and if the time came – when it came – the cats would choose him too. He was one of the saved – if he just committed. Telling Chloe any of that was out of the question, so he said, 'Yeah, it's an incredible opportunity. I'm trying to believe everything that Casper told me, but I guess it takes some time to sink in.'

'It does,' said Chloe with assurance. 'But once you understand it and believe it, it all makes perfect sense. You'd be a fool not to believe.'

He understood that she was giving him an opportunity to affirm his faith, and with it his connection to her. It sounded almost as though she was imploring him. He had never seen her this emotional before. It was weirding him out a bit, so he sucked on his cocktail and tried to appear agreeable.

'Oh yeah, I do believe,' he said, empowered by his conviction that he was only stretching the truth rather than outright lying. 'I just need to internalise it all.'

'Well, you'll be with Casper every day, and you'll hear every lesson he gives, every word he speaks. You'll be there when he proves just how intelligent and insightful cats are, and with luck, you'll be there when the cats return to take us home. If that doesn't make you a true Felinist, I don't know what will.'

'I'm sure it will. I can't wait.' He tried to pump up his enthusiasm levels for her sake.

'Yeah, well, don't fuck it up, Rex. If you do, I'll never forgive you.'

'Don't worry, I won't.' He was certain that after a comment like that, he'd do more than enough worrying for both of them. He wished he could just fall into faith the way she had, and he promised himself he'd work at it.

They ordered an expensive dinner, and Chloe ate like a tiger while Rex picked at his quinoa and duck's tongue risotto or whatever it was. She prattled on about Felinism and what a wonderful time he would have, and how brilliant and intuitive and warm and generous Casper was, and how she wished so much that she was going with them.

When he dropped her off, she asked him in, but at the last moment, at the door, she demurred.

'Oh, I want you to come in Rex,' she said in a whisper, 'but you'd better not. You're travelling with him tomorrow.' If she thought he'd root and tell, he was ready to swear on his 2014 Palmyra Pirates Cricket Club MVP trophy that he would not. But he suspected that it was the thought of *him* that stopped her from going all the way, and that hurt. Whatever the reason, the moment was past. She wrapped her arms around him and gave him a long, sloppy, wet kiss on the mouth – no tongue, much to his disappointment – and said, 'I'll miss you, Rexy. Take care of him, and take care of yourself. I want to see you both back here, good friends and very successful, soon. Bye.'

And then she disappeared behind the closed door, and he was confused and randy. He drove home slowly, thinking about Chloe, cats, Casper and fate, and when he got there, he realised he'd better pack up his house if he was going to leave it locked up for an indefinite period.

He worked into the night, emptying the fridge, putting various items in storage, checking locks and making sure the place would survive his absence without too much hassle. He was physically and emotionally exhausted by the time he'd finished, but he was ready to go.

23. Cats are calculating

Expending energy unnecessarily is not in a cat's nature. Everything a cat does is to advance some agenda, even if that is only to amuse themselves. When a cat is being nice to you, that's the time to be most on your guard, to look into their motives and to see where you fit into their intentions. To be more like a cat, plan your game several moves ahead.

Casper

The long, white limo pulled up in front of The Gallery right on sunset. First out was Rex, wearing a new, tight-fitting black suit with a dark grey shirt, wrap-around sunnies and a short haircut, also new. He stood at attention by the car door he'd just opened as Casper stepped out.

Paris had marshalled a small crowd of eager Felinists and potential groupies outside, and they all clapped and aaaahed appreciatively when they saw Casper. He was, as always, dressed in pure white, his gauzy shirt open halfway to the navel in spite of the autumn coolness sweeping down from the hills that guard the city. He waved and smiled for the admiring gaggle, and with Rex at his side ushering people out of the way, they followed him as he strode towards the door, his head held high and proud. Coco and Yuki, who'd gotten out of the car behind Casper, were lost in the mob.

As he passed Paris, Casper spoke out of the side of his mouth, loud enough that only she – and Rex, who was walking with him – could hear.

'What the fuck is this place? Looks like a second-rate graffiti hangout. And next time, get a better crowd.' Then he walked into the place beaming like he'd just coughed up a giant hairball right in the middle of the bed.

Paris bowed her head until he'd gone inside. The Gallery was one of the hippest, artiest places in hip, arty Adelaide, and she knew that once he realised that, he would calm down. When he was nervous, as he usually was before any function in a new place, he often lashed her with some sort of petty criticism. She was used to it.

Rex took up his station by the door, watching everyone who came in and went out, looking menacing, distant and alert by turns. The event was a meet and greet for the Adelaide faithful – people who had already contributed significant sums to the cult's coffers and could be counted on to level up to the elite echelon and help spread the cat word. A couple of friendly journalists were also in attendance, vetted and groomed by Paris as was standard practice.

As he stood being as impassive and impressive as he could, Rex meditated on Paris. Even though they'd only been on the road for a day or so, that wasn't the first time Rex had seen the Cat Man spit his chewy at her, in an idiomatic sense – even Casper wouldn't expectorate a chewed wad of gum. In spite of her hard work, diligence and supreme tolerance, Paris bore the brunt of Casper's worst tempers and most childish tantrums, always coming back for more and never wavering in her devotion. It occurred to Rex that, far from being the cat she tried with such diligence to be, Paris might have been more of a dog, like him, in her constancy and fidelity. Then again, she made a lot of things happen quickly and with minimum fuss, which he had come to regard as catlike behaviour. Maybe she was the perfect mix of the two, able to channel cattish power and canine doggedness at will.

She was the engine of the organisation in many ways, and it was odd but perhaps inevitable that Casper would come to resent the one he relied on so much. Sometimes he was so nasty to her that Rex began to suspect that she might even be family. That would also explain why he never slept with her, which made her the odd girl out. But she had a different last name, so it was anyone's guess. There was much about the Cat Man, his entourage and his church that was nigh on impossible to fathom.

Over the next three hours, Casper schmoozed and flattered the gathered, touching forearms with the daintiest application of a sensuous fingertip, surreptitiously patting behinds, waving his wispy hair around, and flashing his toothy smile with casual brilliance. His targets were almost exclusively the ladies, and if they were accompanied by male partners, he unleashed his most important weapons on them: Yuki and Coco.

These two, as Rex discovered, were not just comely embellishments to the Felinist cause. Their primary purpose was to bubble around Casper in public looking sensational and saying little, but there were times when the boss had snared some rich lady and convinced her to buy into the story, but whose partner needed 'nurturing.' At those times, Coco and Yuki deployed fine catlike qualities and exquisite predatory skills, toying with the prey until he was ready to sign over large chunks of his fortune, or at least to attend a meeting to discuss the possibility, for the price of a smile. The rest of the time, stunning, vibrant and playful as they were, Coco and Yuki remained virtually invisible to Casper.

That first big event in Adelaide set a pattern of sorts. Rex was constantly on call, and almost always at his boss's side. There were times when he had to stand guard at meetings, press conferences where he had to herd the press into and out of the Presence, and now and then a vaguely threatening situation in which someone threw a hissy fit, or some bogan thought he might make a name by taking on the Cat Man. These he defused quickly and easily, drawing admiring attention for his authority, coolness and raffish good looks. Often he was compelled – oh, the travail of it all – to spend long hours in the vivacious company of Coco and Yuki.

During those early days on the road, the enigma that was Casper himself deepened for Rex. He was alternately exhausted, irritated, radiant, confident, stressed, cheerful, hilarious, effusive, sullen, sarcastic, evasive, instructive, maudlin, gregarious, introspective and conceited, depending on how much effort he'd had to put in, how easily his charm had worked, and how many catnaps he'd taken along the way. When they were alone, Casper surprised Rex by being open, confiding and even entertaining. He furnished a great deal of detail, often bizarre but somehow all the more credible for that, of the Great Experiment. He described the appearance and personality of Muit, supreme leader of the planet Meon; he talked about the Bubastis, the spacecraft that brought the cats to earth; and he told personal anecdotes about its commander, Freyja. He even mentioned the day of the week that they arrived – a Friday, later so named after the commander of the vessel, the first cat to be revered as a god. Stuff that, as Rex reckoned it, was so weird, so beyond imagining, that it couldn't have been made up.

The fourth day of the tour, consisting of many meet and greets, two full-blown receptions, a number of private meetings with well-heeled donors, and the inevitable visit to a cat refuge, was a long one. He hadn't yet developed that fitness peculiar to standing still all day, and at the end of it, he was wrecked. The hours spent watching his boss being variously cruel, sweet, charming, intellectual, preening, prissy and adorable – depending on who he was talking to and who was watching – had taken its toll.

Back in his room, he took off his shoes, unbuttoned his shirt and his pants, and sat back on his comfy couch studying the room-service menu. There hadn't been a lot of time to eat during the day, and he wasn't allowed to tuck into the extravagant spreads Paris had organised at every stop, so he was hungry enough to eat the crotch out of a low flying duck. He was just deciding whether to have the spaghetti bolognese, the chicken parmigiana or both, when his phone rang. Chloe!

'Hello.' He'd wanted it to sound alert, positive, assured; but there was an unexpected bark in it. He wondered if he could blame a bad line?

'Rexy,' she said. At the very sound of her voice, his brain self-combusted and the warmth from the fire coursed through his system. 'How's my favourite bouncer?'

'I'm not a bouncer; I'm head of security.' His indignation was only partially mock – was she playing with him or just amusing herself? No matter; he was picturing her in his mind, lying on a sofa, or better yet a bed. All stretched out and supple, her hair somehow perfect, artfully arranged on a pillow, her eyes sparkling clear and her lips full and red. No doubt wearing something sheer, and in his mind's eye so delicate and translucent that it might as well not have been there at all.

'Sure you are, sweetie. Sure you are.'

He made a strange, grunting sound, and her voice changed gear, as though she was aware that she perhaps sounded a little too sexy, and she wanted to move things on. 'So, how's life on the road?' she asked in a brighter, brisker tone. 'Are you loving it?'

'Ah, yeah, it's all right so far. Hard work, but not too bad, I s'pose.'

'Come on, you big fibber. It's awesome and you know it. All those pretty girls, all those ritzy hotels. You must be having a ball.'

He didn't want her to get the idea that he was tomcatting his way across the country; that would be counterproductive.

'I'm a professional,' he said. 'I don't have time to muck around. Besides, all those pretty girls don't even know I exist. Their eyes are only for Casper.' He hadn't meant to throw a dart, but he knew that he had as soon as he said it. There was a long pause, and he realised it had struck home.

'You're so lucky,' she said, 'being at his side all the time. You must be learning so much.'

He couldn't deny it. 'I s'pose,' he said.

'And how is he? He's not working too hard, is he? Not skipping meals? Spreading himself too thin?'

For the next ten minutes, the conversation – like Chloe's world and now his – revolved around Casper. She wanted to know everything: who he spoke to, what events they held and where, how many people went, how many new members they'd signed up, who Casper slept with and how often, how he looked, how he sounded, what he wore. And so on and so on. When she had gleaned as much information as she could and could tell that Rex was tiring of the inquisition, she backed off.

'Oh, well,' she said by way of a sign-off. 'I'd better let you go, darling. I just wanted to see how you were.'

Bullshit, he said to himself after she'd hung up. *She just wanted to know how fucking Casper is.* The same bloke who in all likelihood was at that very moment madly rooting some random cat lover. Still, she'd called *him* to find out, hadn't she? That had to count for something. He was still on her radar somewhere.

He knew it was pathetic. He was disgusted at himself for being so desperate. But he didn't care. He'd spoken to Chloe, he'd heard the lilt in her voice and he could pretend that her concern had been for him. And he'd had that vision of her, lying all stretched out and supple, and that would just have to be enough. It was. The food order could wait another five minutes.

24. Cats are mercenary

There isn't much a cat won't do to attain its ambitions. It will swallow contempt and cosy up to the person or object least likely in the world to attract it, if doing so gets it closer to its goal of world domination. Never waste an opportunity, no matter how far beneath you it appears. It may be the key to your future, and it will certainly make you more like a cat.

Casper

Hissing, whining and petulant peevishness issued from the back seat of the limo as they drove up into the Adelaide hills. 'Why do I have to go and see some horrible old lady?' Casper was bleating. 'An old bag who smells of cat piss and sherry. She'll probably want to touch me. Ewwww.' He shuddered theatrically.

'Mrs Firth loves cats, she adores Felinism and she's desperate to meet you,' said Paris. She carried the imperturbable equanimity of a queen Siamese sitting on a plush velvet cushion. Getting Casper to accept the inevitable was often an uphill battle, but she fought on because she knew that sooner or later, she would win. She was as much of a cat as he was in many ways, and was content to play him at his own, niggling game. If they got to the place and he was still resisting, she could always just order him to do it, and he would comply. But it would never come to that, because his inherent insatiability would come to the fore before that became necessary. He knew what was at stake here.

'Also, she has a cat that she wants to give us for a Cat Life Centre. This is our opportunity to meet Bailey and assess whether he would be comfortable living with other cats.'

'Great, so now I'm giving fucking job interviews to cats,' Casper snarled.

Rex was unimpressed by this grating performance. After just a few days on the road, he was starting to realise that their trip would not be all groupies and free pizzas. As the moaning droned on, he fell to musing about Chloe. What might she think of the great Cat Man if she saw him carrying on this way? He sighed as he realised that she would give him a pass.

Casper was right about one thing: our creations control us rather than the other way around, and that extends to the ideas we form and the stories we tell ourselves to rationalise them. Chloe had fashioned an idea – or rather an ideal – of Casper, and she would overlook any obnoxious, objectionable or distasteful personality traits that didn't support that romantic vision. His prickly side would tickle rather than spike her, and she would find his childish side cute rather than puerile. His nasty side, to which Rex was becoming more exposed, she would dismiss as the product of overwork or extreme provocation, as it was impossible for her to believe that Casper could be brutal or insensitive.

He sighed and tried to block out the endless spiteful belly-aching, watching the landscape blur past his window.

'How much has she given us so far?'

'Well not so much yet, but she's very rich, quite old and has no family. So behave yourself.'

The limo drove through a pair of iron gates set in a high, wide, hedged wall, and crackled down a long, curling gravel driveway. It was obvious that the expansive gardens on either side had once been trimmed, swept and pampered to immaculate beauty, and though much of their former grandeur remained, overgrowth, leaf piles and weeds marred the magnificence. The groundsman was probably as old as the mistress of the house, and less inclined to care.

As they pulled up, Rex saw a tall, previously majestic portico of white marble with fluted columns flanking worn stairs, the entrance to a manor of lost elegance that retained a sense of dignity despite advancing dilapidation. They got out and were admitted into the home by a fresh, young retainer who introduced herself as Elizabet.

Rex saw Casper grimace when she explained that no, there was no H on the end; it was just Elizabet. He shared with his boss a visceral aversion to the contemporary trend of creating ridiculous new names, or corrupting perfectly good old ones, with the intention of creating some sort of individuality for the child so encumbered. It wasn't hard to like the boss sometimes.

Elizabet led the three of them upstairs, the house getting darker and the smell getting mustier the deeper into it they delved. Still, there was a faded elegance about the place, and above and beyond the stuffy mustiness there was an overwhelming aura of money. The artworks on the walls, the huge vases and the teak and walnut tables on which they stood, the fittings on the doors and lights – everything was old and out of fashion, unchanged since who knew when, but even a philistine like Rex could see it was all of the very highest quality. The hallway alone could take up an entire episode of Antiques Roadshow, and Rex could imagine the experts' eyes popping out when they saw some of the items that had been locked away in this time capsule for decades.

'Mrs Firth is confined to her room, and has been for some time,' said Elizabet. 'But don't let that fool you; she is as sharp as ever, and quite the conversationalist.' Casper marshalled a smile and a little bow.

'I'm sure she's delightful,' he said.

They were ushered into the room, which, unlike the stairs and hallway they had just negotiated, was flooded with light, free of that mildewy thickness of air, and only faintly redolent of medicine and brandy. Every surface shone or sparkled, and the opulence of the furnishings was like an assault. Casper brightened as he took in the scene and calculated the value of the property and the lady before him.

Mrs Firth sat in a high-backed rosewood chair with ornate carvings and thick leather padding. The sunlight streamed in through an open French window and bounced off countless crystals and mirrored surfaces. Beaming, Mrs Firth held out a thin, bony hand with a single, large diamond on one finger and a pearl bracelet around the equally bony wrist. She wore a soft cotton shirt with lace trimmings, and her legs were hidden beneath a light silk blanket. Her broad smile showed perfect dentures, and her face, though heavily made-up, showed a legion of wrinkles and laugh lines. There was a slight yellowness in the whites of her eyes and a little extra sag in the bottom eyelids, but her colour was otherwise good and her expression bright.

'Mrs Firth, this is Mr Casper White, his assistant Ms Paris Selkirk, and their, um … Mr Rex Shepherd.'

In an instant, Casper was across the room, grasping the gaunt, scrawny hand and smothering it in both of his, putting his face close enough to hers to kiss it without actually going that far.

'Mrs Firth of Firth Glass?' he asked with an innocent, almost hesitant smile, as though this was the first time he'd heard the name and made the obvious connection. Firth Glass had been the bottle suppliers to South Australia's premium winegrowers since the very beginning of the industry there in the mid-nineteenth century, and the business had spread not just across Australia but to the prime growing regions of South Africa and the United States. It was a massive multinational, remarkably still under the control of a single family, of which Mrs Firth was the sole and final representative – and she was in the process of selling. She nodded and smiled with pride.

The Casper of the car was gone, and in his place there came a fawning, servile flatterer who seemed to have dialled into Mrs Firth's innermost wishes and loves. For the next hour, through several pots of tea, which he normally hated but now claimed to love, he was all over her, throwing out the compliments by the bucketful, abasing himself before her, tittering at her every remark, and being by turns coy, bold and endearing in what appeared to be just the right combination.

He professed to have fallen head over heels in love with Bailey, a mangy old critter who would be eaten alive at the Cat Life Centre and whose destiny, if left in the hands of Casper, would be the green dream. He held the unwilling animal in a firm grip on his lap, trying to pat around the scabs and flecks of drool, and assured Mrs Firth that Bailey would no doubt assume his rightful position as the patriarch of the feline community at the Cat Life Centre he intended to build in Adelaide.

He spoke of the dream he had of making the whole world as cat-friendly and loving as he and his hostess were, and of his despair at being shy of the funds required to make it happen. A few dollars, he implied, was the sole impediment to him making the whole of humanity happy, peaceful cat lovers.

He reeled off the names of celebrities he had met, opining that Mrs Firth would get on famously with Dame Joan Collins, asserting that Robert De Niro was a cat fanatic and member of the church, and letting slip that Betty White had pledged to leave a sizeable chunk of her fortune to furthering the good work of Felinism.

Once he had her thoroughly entranced, Casper slid into unctuous salesman mode without blinking. He again lamented the cost of bringing cat happiness to the world, sighed as he expressed how he wished he could do more but was hamstrung by a lack of money and support, and managed to combine expectation and gratitude into a single look as he implored Mrs Firth to consider leaving the Church of Felinism just a tiny part of her legacy, 'when your time comes, hopefully many years from now.'

Mrs Firth, who was by no means as gullible as she allowed herself to appear, had a small problem. She was possessed of a huge fortune, which was about to grow by an astronomical amount, and a short time in which to dispose of it. Her greatest fear was that the government would take it.

It was obvious from the way she indulged Casper that she liked him, and she gave out that she would be happy to help, as she had plenty to go around. By the time they left, he had secured a signed bequest form for a very generous sum and, to the astonishment of all, a cheque with so many zeroes on it that Casper couldn't hold back a little yelp of pleasured surprise. He grasped the skeletal hands again, planted kisses right on the jowly old cheeks with a perfectly assumed facsimile of sincerity, and grinned like a feline from a well-known Lewis Carroll story.

When the gates of the mansion were behind them and Casper was slumped in his seat like an athlete who'd just won a gold medal, or an actor who knows he's just given an award-winning performance and is exhausted but elated, he said, 'Well, with any luck the old bat will fall off the perch tomorrow.' Then, looking at Bailey, crouched in a cage on the seat next to him and eyeing his new blonde owner with suspicion, he added, 'You, my old mate, won't make it that far.'

25. Cats are thorough

When a cat does something, it does it properly. That native marsupial will be comprehensively dead (and if only partially eaten, it's because not all parts are worthy of the cat's palate), that fur will be licked clean twice over, and that turd will smell like the bowels of hell itself. Everything a cat does, it does to the limit. Be like a cat.

Casper

They spent the remaining seven days of the tour in Adelaide attending receptions and meetings that hummed with an evangelical tenor, and informal get-togethers with supporters, getting to know them and encourage their financial support. Well-attended pressers opened the door to a couple of one-on-one interviews granted to especially attractive young female journalists, one of which resulted in the journalist taking the walk of shame early the next morning as Rex was coming to wake the boss up. He may have been shameless, but the Cat Man had excellent taste.

Affected by a hangover and an irritability-inducing sleep

deficit, that day Casper still managed to conduct a Level Three initiation for a group of eight people – one of three scheduled for the week. Most of the new Level Threes would go on to become operatives for the organisation, but some were inducted purely as cash cows – or cash cats – who would commit generous monthly sums to the upkeep and proliferation of Felinism.

The days, the events and the unending parade of cats and cat people whizzed by, the money mountain grew, and Rex got to know his boss at close quarters through every conceivable scene and mood. Casper was always spoiled by – and often intolerably shitty to – the girls; when he thought no one was watching he treated 'little' people like waiters and hotel personnel as though they didn't exist; he lost no time and showed no shame in sucking up to media personalities and people of money or influence; he was cranky and often easily rankled but just as often serene and detached; and now and then he made a terrible scene just to watch the carnage unfold.

But he was always polite, friendly, even fraternal with Rex, so it was hard for him to be too outraged about the Cat Man's behaviour. The contradiction between Casper's dealings with others and the way he behaved with Rex was not lost on the latter, but when a person presents himself to you as cordial, accommodating and amiable, it's hard to judge them harshly for their failings. Every dog knows that the quickest way to starvation is to bite the hand that feeds.

Having spent a hectic nine days in the City of Churches – and 'walked away with the chocolates,' as Casper giggled – the gang moved on to Melbourne, selected as the next city to be blessed with a Cat Life Centre. The Adelaide centre mentioned to Mrs Firth was, it became clear to Rex, no more than a campaign promise.

From the very first, Casper loved Melbourne. Its laid-back hipster vibe and the attendant attitude of taking a great deal of care to seem not to care at all appealed to him as being quite catlike. He complimented the city on its 'underlying felinity' to anyone that would listen – which encompassed quite a solid slice of a self-absorbed population eager for their egotistical ways to be validated. Rex wondered if there might just be so many cats in Melbourne because there were so many rats to feed on, but he kept that thought to himself.

Beyond the official engagements, hours and hours were spent traipsing in and out of cafes and ingesting gallons of mediocre coffee in the cause of meeting people keen to help, ingratiating financial supporters and scouting for suitable premises for the new Cat Life Centre. Casper drank a lot of milk, played his wrist-lick-to-ear-wash trick with wearisome regularity, and tossed his white-gold locks around a lot. If he loved Melbourne, the city and its media loved him back in spades, and there was hardly a newspaper, online blog or current affairs TV program that didn't laud him to the skies. Rex was kept busy because the Felinist entourage's every move was shadowed by a press and paparazzi contingent, and their demands were as tiring as Casper's back-room tantrums.

A St Kilda site was at last agreed upon for the centre, and there was a flurry of late-night calls to the finance Dobermann in California, afternoons consumed poring over the plans that Rex hurriedly drew up, and mornings spent pleading poor with local builders, to get a better deal. The idea was to use Rex's design in Subiaco as the model, so he was co-opted to lead the fit-out team, an assignment he relished.

Casper had already selected his preferred manager for the Melbourne Cat Life Centre, a fit young feline named Penny who wore her hair in pigtails and bounced around like a kitten. Penny's elevation to Level Three, a prerequisite to her assuming a managerial role, was conducted in Casper's suite on a Saturday afternoon, while Rex stood outside waiting to take the boss to his next appointment. This particular initiation appeared to have been much more thorough than his own, judging from the bestial racket emanating from the room, and once it was consummated Casper and Penny emerged looking hot, flushed and freshly showered.

Not every recruit enjoyed the same treatment – if they had, Casper would have exhausted himself on the constant stream of pretty young things that joined the team over the next few weeks. While Rex supervised the construction and fitting of the new Cat Life Centre, a cast of baristas, servers, cooks, veterinary assistants and animal handlers was assembled, and along with them a herd of kittens and cats to populate it. Whether cat or cashier, the selection criteria were the same – the appointee must be beautiful, delightful, self-assured and devoted to the Cat Man. It was astounding just how many of these gorgeous creatures fitted that description, and after a short, intensive operation, an entire staff and cat complement was ready to go.

But the recruitment didn't stop there. The Cat Man's entourage expanded to cover the increased workload. Paris took on a young assistant, Oscar; Coco and Yuki were joined by Izzy, Skye and – in the interests of equality – Sebastian; and Rex was given two assistants, Mickey and Gus. The growing retinue worked well together, and Mickey and Gus took a lot of the pressure off Rex. He was still the only one to provide personal protection to the boss at critical times, and the two assistants were intended never to progress beyond Level One, but it meant that he had backup if he needed it. At least he had someone to carry his bags, as opposed to carrying everyone else's, and he was free to concentrate on the Cat Life Centre project.

In one sense, Rex was relieved to be on-site all day rather than spending his time standing around looking fierce, watching Casper seamlessly segue from being a shit to a schmoozer and back again. Some distance from the Cat Man and the girls was welcome at first, because it gave him time to consider his relationship with them all and with the church. But after just a few days, he found he missed being at the eye of the storm with Casper. Worse, he missed Casper himself, and found himself downplaying the boss's infuriating habits and reminiscing over the blokey camaraderie that had come from their being the only two men in that gaggle of beautiful but sometimes exasperating girls. Not having the girls themselves around to harass, tease and joke with him, as well as to provide entertaining arguments, gossip and an atmosphere of enlivening loveliness, made life quiet indeed.

Even from his position on the periphery, he was across all the recruitment, and he saw how thrilled all the newcomers were to be a part of something so revolutionary and mind-blowing, and in many of them he could discern genuine catlike tendencies and traits. It made him want to be a part of it rather than alongside it, and by the time the Melbourne centre was set to open, he was ready to rejoin the troupe. In quiet moments at work during the build, he even found himself contemplating the divinity of cats and the possibility that he would one day be spirited away to the cat planet, and being excited by the prospect.

The opening was a blazing success, with a positive inferno of attendant publicity, and for Rex it was fabulous to be back amongst it, watching the master at work and seeing how effectively each member of the team played their different roles. By the end of the night, it seemed that Casper had personally touched every guest – most in a literal sense – and created an authentic buzz around the cafe and his church.

As they drove away and the Cat Man flaked, blissful but bushed, in the back of the limo, Rex couldn't help but admire his thoroughness.

26. Cats have claws

Cats don't hear no. You can ask, order, implore and plead with a cat not to do something and they will ignore you. You're not the boss of them, and if they want to puke all over the carpet, tear up the couch, spray on the walls – or worse – they can, and you'll just have to deal with it. And if you have a problem with that, the claws will come out. Be more like a cat.

Casper

Winter had been closing in on the east coast of Australia for some time, and by the time the troupe was installed in a suite of rooms and an executive penthouse for Casper, it had struck. The waters of Sydney Harbour, which would ordinarily spread out in twinkling blue majesty before them, were shrouded in dense, raging curtains of rain, and a fierce squall whipped up a short, foamy chop.

It was entertaining just to watch the ferries, which will venture out in all but the most cyclonic of conditions, trying to navigate in and out of tiny Circular Quay. The Opera House, just a few hundred metres away on the other side of the quay, could barely be seen in the gloom, its sails riding the storm like a ghost ship. The mighty Sydney Harbour Bridge almost directly over their heads caught the wind and made it whistle and howl.

The mood in the upper echelons of Felinism was un-dampened. Melbourne had been a phenomenal success, and the media down there couldn't get enough of Casper and his fabulous looks, his well-honed maxims about how marvellous it is to be a cat, and his retinue of gorgeous acolytes. There was no reason to suspect that Sydney would be any different.

Paris and Oscar, the handsome young media graduate she had hired in Melbourne, had worked up quite a relaxed schedule for the first week or so. Casper even spent a couple of days incommunicado, catching up with family and old friends who were delighted to share in his success. So there was, when the weather permitted, plenty of sightseeing and even more hard partying in the area around the hotel – the luxury joint in the Rocks where they were holed up was ideal for all sorts of culinary and nocturnal high jinks.

Rex wished at every turn that Chloe was there to see it with him. Alas, he had to settle for escorting the gaggle of girls – and girlish Sebastian – around town, getting into posh clubs for free, and watching them get free drinks everywhere. He spent most nights staring at his phone wishing Chloe would call, and when she did, wishing she would talk about some-thing other than Casper.

A few days in, the weather began to stay clear for longer spurts, and the sphere of activities broadened. The search for a home for the new Sydney Cat Life Centre began in earnest. Casper, Paris, Oscar and Rex tramped the streets of the CBD, North Sydney, Double Bay, Potts Point,

Newtown, Kings Cross, Bondi Junction and Bondi Beach seeking that perfect blend of hipster cachet, money, class and gullibility, which was harder to find than Rex had imagined. They sipped a million lattes, munched their way through a mountain of muffins and swallowed, with a certain amount of reluctance in Rex's case, a truckload of quinoa this or kale that. At night, Casper and Paris, with Coco, Yuki, Skye, Rex, Sebastian and Oscar, or some combination thereof, entertained the people who were to be coaxed into paying for it all. They ate at upper-class restaurants that served unpronounceable dishes at indigestible prices, and usually finished with late-night debauches in Casper's eyrie.

It was at one of these nocturnal hunts, a sundowner overlooking the surf in Bondi, that Tilly first sashayed onto the scene. The moment he saw her, Rex knew the fascinating young lady heading towards the door he was watching would be Casper's next trophy and earthly representative in Sydney.

Tilly exuded the kind of energy that said she was born a cat. There was an easy athleticism about her walk, her shoulders held proudly forward and her head high. Yet there was still much of the kitten about her, and she seemed unaffected by her immense beauty and poise, so there was an aura of innocent newness about her. Unlike most other cat women, Tilly didn't dress to emphasise her feline grace; she wore short, short shorts and a simple tank top, and her dark auburn hair was braided into pigtails so that she looked very young and naive. Rex hoped looks were deceiving, because if she was as innocent as she seemed, Casper would eat her up. Even Rex, who was almost inured to the endless parade of sexy young things that Casper seemed to draw out of the woodwork, was stunned at her freshness and vitality, not to mention the magnetic sensuality that practically rubbed off on him as she brushed past him and into the cocktail party.

Tilly had been employed to work in the new Cat Life Centre just off Campbell Parade, not far from where the party was being held at Bondi Icebergs. Initially, Paris and Oscar had interviewed her and agreed to put her on staff, but as soon as Casper saw her, he pegged her for a position closer to his orbit. He spotted her from across the room and almost lost his composure. Here was a treasure he must make his own. He extricated himself from the conversation he'd been having through the simple expedient of walking away, leaving the couple he'd been charming disconcerted but accepting. He was a cat, after all, and they'd seen the tasty target walk into the room too.

As much as he could from his location at the door, Rex watched the chase unfold. He thought Tilly was perhaps a bit less taken with the boss than almost every other fan he'd met or seen on the trip. Sure, she was curious, as is the way with cats, but not entirely captivated.

If ever there was a demeanour calculated to drive the Cat Man wild, that was it. The whole night, Casper stalked Tilly with sly, skulking vanity. He cornered her whenever he could and cooed at her, pushing his other adoring adherents away whenever she was near and doing all he could to monopolise her attention. If she was playing a game, Tilly played it perfectly. She even affected boredom at one stage, slipping away by ducking under the outstretched arm by which he'd almost pinned her to a wall, and heading into the girls' room. The lust in his eyes and the frustration on his face were plain to see. Less noticeable was the predacious determination that one way or another he would get his claws into her.

As the evening drew to a close and the crowd was starting to leave in dribs and drabs, Tilly made for the door. Catching her before she left, just a few feet from Rex's big, pricked up ears, Casper threw the biggest bait he could think of – managing the Cat Life Centre in Bondi. Her round eyes showing genuine surprise at this unexpected honour, Tilly blushed and said no thanks; she didn't feel she was experienced enough for the role. There was something in her face that said she suspected the Cat Man's motives. Rex saw it, but so did Casper. Swearing sincerity and effusing enthusiasm, Casper begged her to attend a private interview the next day at his hotel. Tilly, bemused but flattered, accepted. An 'appointment' was duly set up for the early afternoon.

When she heard about Casper's plan, Paris was annoyed because she'd arranged a luncheon with some heavy donors, and she gave him a hard, dark look of misgiving. But there was nothing she could do – Casper was adamant that he needed very much to discuss the Bondi Cat Life Centre with Tilly and get her on-board.

Rex and Casper left the lunch early and returned to the hotel, where Tilly was waiting in the lobby. In the daylight, she seemed less sure of herself, and of Casper, but no less dramatically striking. Behind her nervous eyes, Rex saw a resolve to at least go through with the interview, but it seemed to him that 'no' was already written all over her face. Perhaps Casper's reputation had preceded him. They all went up to the suite, and as usual Rex was posted at the door.

To Rex's consternation, this assignation did not unfold as many others like it had. At first there was the usual murmuring talk behind the door, but after a while it erupted into angry words. The quarrel escalated further into shouts and the sounds of physical violence – things being smashed, things falling over and being moved, and then a strange quiet. Unsure of what to do, Rex stood guard as he was paid to do, and tried not to contemplate the scene inside. He tried to imagine that that was just the way things were between those two, but inside of him, a queasy feeling was growing. He let it gnaw at him for a full minute. Fucking Casper, he said to himself. He can't be fucking trusted.

He was about to start bashing on the door and demand to know what was going on when it opened. Tilly emerged from the room shaking, bleeding from a minor cut above the eye, and holding a torn top together.

'He's an animal!' she hissed as she lurched down the hall, unsteady on her feet and sobbing. He was about to go after her and find out what the hell had happened when Casper appeared at the door and grabbed his arm.

'Let her go,' he said. There was venom in his voice that Rex had never heard before, and it sent a chill up his spine. 'Fucking rat bitch,' he said as she got into the lift. As the doors closed, he dabbed at the blood issuing from a line of three fingernail marks across his cheek.

27. Cats always land on their feet

It's a cliché and an article of faith: cats land on their feet, no matter how far they fall or how many twists and turns they perform on the way down. What that means is that no situation can defeat a cat, and very few developments even faze most felines; they can charm, bluff or excite their way out of even the tightest of corners. Be more like a cat.

Casper

Hard on the heels of Tilly's distressed departure, Paris showed up as if by magic, clearly responding to Casper's urgent summons. He let her in by cracking the door open just enough for her to squeeze through, and as she walked in Rex heard her gasp.

The door muffled their conversation, but it was heated, with Paris starting proceedings by going on the attack. Rex thought he heard the word 'again' a couple of times, and definitely heard Paris say 'bitch' at least once. Casper responded by roaring with anger at Paris, at his victim, at his life and the whole motherfucking world. The timing couldn't have been worse, as he was due to record an interview with Daisy Garland, a 60 Minutes journalist, the next day.

The argy-bargy didn't last long, and in the quiet that followed, Rex guessed that Paris must have been attending to Casper's wounds. He doubted there was anything she could do about the damage to his ego, but if he was being honest with himself, he was more concerned about Tilly. He hoped she would be okay, because she'd looked terrified, hurt and angry when she'd bolted down the hall.

Half an hour later, Paris came out and quizzed Rex about what he'd heard and seen. As he related his fragment of the story, including the strange noises and shouting that had preceded Tilly's tearful exit, she kept a deep frown on her face. She made him swear that he'd keep his mouth shut about it, and to let her know if he ever saw Tilly again. Then she brightened – a trifle artificially, as though someone had thrown a switch or turned the dimmer up from minimum to maximum – and said, 'Well, the good news is we've cancelled the rest of the appointments for the day, so you can go and relax.'

Dismissed, Rex went back to his room and lay on his bed, thinking about his boss. The episode with Tilly had shaken him. His belief in Felinism and its origins was beginning to become almost instinctive, and this had been accompanied by a positive view of Casper as a person and as a leader. Seeing the callous violence he'd perpetrated on poor Tilly, and the distant, almost pitiless way in which Paris had dealt with it – as though she'd seen it all before and acted as though it could only have been Tilly's fault – was a wake-up call. Could such an extraordinary vision of the truth as the Great Experiment have been gifted to people with such questionable morals?

By morning, Rex had moved on. Maybe Tilly had forced Casper into the situation. Maybe she had attacked him. Sure, he could be bad-tempered and his insults could be cruel, but he had never seen Casper get violent before. He didn't know the exact circumstances, so it was unfair to judge the scene on what he thought he knew – he may have been wrong about the whole deal.

There was no time during the day to contemplate it, or to talk to Casper about it; they were on the go from early on. The shooting schedule with Daisy began in a cat refuge, then took in the site of the new Cat Life Centre in Bondi. The wrap-up interview was to be conducted in the cosy confines of Casper's suite. There was a lot of hustle and movement, the producer was even bossier than Paris, and there was a horde of people and bits of equipment to keep an eye on.

Daisy reminded Rex of a poodle. She had tight curls the colour of dirty straw, a narrow face with a long, slender nose and lips that were thin but not mean, and eyes of a deep, dark green. She fawned on and played up to her subject, let him answer at his leisure on any and all subjects, and positively glowed when she saw the way he interacted with cats.

'It's like you have so much love and respect for them – and they for you,' she said as she watched Casper cuddle a little moggy at the cat refuge. The animal loved the attention, and Casper knew where to tickle and stroke to get the cutest, most blissed out reaction.

'Of course,' he replied. 'Cats have been a part of our human family since the very first day we stopped wandering and started settling into villages, towns and cities. Even before then, in fact.' His eyes twinkled as if he held some wonderful secret.

'And yet…' Daisy looked meaningfully at the three parallel scratch marks that marred Casper's otherwise flawless visage. They had become quite angry, and in spite of the voluminous application of television pancake, were easily discernible.

'Oh, this? Daisy, you know I have an incredible rapport with cats, and we understand and admire each other. But we cats – I count myself an honorary feline, you know – are volatile, and we're competitive, and sometimes we feel the need to assert ourselves. This,' he said, reaching up to pat his cheek, 'stems from a misunderstanding. But rest assured the pussy involved in this is no longer under any illusions as to who is actually the boss.'

Daisy laughed and congratulated him on his honesty, which she said was 'refreshing.'

Across the day and the locations, Daisy posed few even mildly difficult questions, and gave Casper more than sufficient opportunities to skite about himself, to talk up Felinism and its 'achievements,' to lambast his critics, and to promote his on-line and offline businesses. There were one or two half-hearted attempts at what might pass for hard-hitting journalism, but even these were just gateways to self-aggrandisement.

They were sitting on a comfortable antique lounge in Casper's elegant suite, coming down the home straight, and he was very relaxed. He had Daisy eating out of his hands – quite literally when he smeared caviar on a wafer and fed it to her while she giggled. Going against the flow, she said, 'There are odd rumours about what people who reach the top levels of Felinism are taught. What can you tell us?'

Without even blinking, Casper stared into Daisy's eyes, his gaze cool and compelling. 'I can tell you that I have discovered a beautiful, inescapable truth, Daisy. Felinism is a portal into the very origins of humans and our ultimate destiny, and a series of lessons in how to live life. I would suggest that if you wish to know the true teachings of Felinism, you start by becoming more like a cat. I can teach you, you know. But until you become a high-level practitioner, try not to believe everything you hear.'

The suggestion appeared to agree with Daisy, but she stuck, however briefly, to her guns.

'Is there anything weird in it? I've heard some stories about aliens…'

He laughed, licked the back of his wrist and rubbed it behind his ear. 'Well, I can tell you one thing,' he said. 'It doesn't involve any little green men.' And his smile was so disarming, and his crystalline blue eyes were so mesmeric, that she could do nothing but laugh along with him and seem embarrassed at having asked such a direct question. The next question, like so many of the others she'd asked that day, began with a preamble along the lines of 'You've attained such incredible success and amazing results in the few years you've been teaching Felinism to the world…'

Casper sat back and smiled, and sipped his milk.

28. Cats are stone cold killers

Go ahead, fuck with a cat. Or simply fail to anticipate their needs. See how that works out for you. You'll have your eyes ripped out and your guts spilled all over the yard. Because you're only good to a cat as long as you show total fealty, readiness to serve and absolute forgiveness of their sins. If you want to inspire loyalty and rule the world, be more like a cat.

Casper

A few days later the *60 Minutes* story ran, and the cat – or rather, the Cat Man – had got the cream. Where Casper and Felinism had been a curiosity before, they were now instantly the next big thing: the craze that everyone wanted to taste and many savoured. The online stats went crazy as hundreds and then thousands of people sniffed, pawed and licked Felinism, and decided that they wanted more.

Chloe told Rex that business in the Subiaco Cat Life Centre had trebled overnight, and Level One memberships were up by a factor of five. Coyly, she suggested that though Casper must be busy, this was the kind of news it would be cruel to keep from him. She would have told him herself, she said, but for some reason she was having trouble getting through to him. Maybe he'd lost his phone and got a new one, or maybe he was busy and Paris was gatekeeping for him – who knew? She'd tossed this off with a light, dismissive tone, but Rex could tell it was annoying the crap out of her. He promised he'd pass it on.

For the next week, every event was packed, and Rex and Mickey and Gus had their work cut out just controlling the boisterous, brimming crowds. Media vans followed them everywhere, and Rex had to remove several press and TV crews from places where private conversations about substantial donations and ongoing commitments were being conducted, directing them and their cameras to the spots where neophytes were being signed up in fervent droves.

'Big things, Rex,' a beaming Casper said one afternoon as they were on their way from a private club lunch in North Sydney to a cat rescue mission for a photo opportunity. 'I've cancelled Brisbane.'

As they crossed the harbour, the giant steel Meccano set that is the Sydney Harbour Bridge flickered the light, sending Rex into a near-hypnotic trance as he stared down at an incoming passenger liner. It had only been a few weeks since they'd left Perth, and he'd talked with Chloe almost every day – granted, about Casper most of the time – but Rex was missing her. He'd been thinking about when he might get home to visit her, or when she might come and see him. If she did, she could see Casper, which would no doubt appeal.

'Huh?' he said.

'Do listen, old boy,' said Casper. His present good nature could not be flapped by Rex's habitual inattention. 'I've cancelled Brisbane. We're staying in Sydney.'

'Eh?'

'The *60 Minutes* thing went so well we've had to bring some of our plans forward. In addition to the Bondi Cat Life Centre, we're looking at one in Kings Cross and a third in Darling Harbour. We've got to get busy, mate.'

'Wow.' Some days, monosyllabism was the best Rex could do. But at least now he was paying closer attention.

'We're moving to a house in Potts Point – all of us. Well, except for those doggy mates of yours, Mickey and Gus. They can go get a flat in Kings Cross or something. Paris and the finance Dobermann are working on the details right now. It's a big motherfucker of a house with all the shit we need, including good office space. It'll be the new Felinism world headquarters.'

'Wow,' said Rex again. There was a note of sadness in his voice now, or at least distant disappointment. It would be some time before he got home, then.

The mansion overlooking Elizabeth Bay was indeed a big motherfucker, but it was fully furnished, so moving in was a doddle. Casper had an entire wing to himself, and Paris a room of her own. Coco and Yuki shared a room, as did Skye and Izzy. The original plan was for Rex to share a room with Oscar and Sebastian, but he was not keen. He was, he explained to Paris, a solitary individual, and wanted his own space.

He solved the problem by volunteering to sleep in the tiny guesthouse out by the pool. It was cramped and less than luxurious, but had its own bathroom, and it gave him a sense of freedom and independence. Best of all, it didn't cost him a cent. He loved curling up on his blanket at night and dropping off to sleep dreaming of Chloe.

Sebastian and Oscar hid their disappointment.

With the change in environment came a change in

atmosphere. They were no longer on tour, and settled into a more workaday rhythm. There were fewer events and gatherings, but a similar level of busyness. Casper got back to the grind of being a cult leader: writing inspiring blogs and motivational tracts, shooting videos for the online channels, and spending a lot of time thinking with his eyes closed. Rex was not the only one to find this contemplation indistinguishable from napping, and they all knew not to interrupt the boss when he was meditating thus.

'Great news, Rexy,' said Casper the day after they'd all moved in. 'You're going back to what you love.'

For a heartbeat, Rex hoped he meant Perth, and Chloe, but that would be too good to be true, and besides, he was fairly sure Casper had no idea of his feelings for her. He pricked up his ears and raised an eyebrow to show he was listening.

'Building,' said Casper with a grin. 'With the Bondi Cat Life Centre on the go, and two more to start as soon as possible, it's all hands on deck. I want you to supervise the design and construction.'

'Strewth.' Rex was genuinely chuffed. It was all he could do not to puff out his chest, and for once he wished he had a tail, just so he could wag it. There were times when being a real dog would have its upside.

'With a healthy pay rise, of course.'

'Mate!'

'And a new title. You're the construction supervisor of the Oceania chapter of Felinism. Congratulations, mate.'

Not knowing what to say but smiling so wide he was in danger of splitting a cheek, Rex bowed his head and tucked his shirt in properly.

The first week and then fortnight flew by. Everyone in

the Cat House, as it became known, had their own tasks and agendas, and all were thoroughly invested in growing their church.

Coco, Yuki, Sebastian, Skye and Izzy each ran their own team of street hustlers who gave out pamphlets and videos, chatted to people about cats, and invited anyone who showed the slightest interest to a free lecture. Presented twice a week by Paris, Coco or Yuki, these lectures featured funny and adorable cat videos, and a watered-down version of the Level One induction designed to kindle interest in Felinism. Any personable young ladies or men the street team thought would be good Cat Life Centre or church workers were invited to separate, more intimate sessions, which were held once a fortnight and personally delivered by Casper.

It was a busy time for everyone, and the number of people coming and going was phenomenal. It seemed that the church was growing at an exponential rate. Rex didn't have to pay too much attention to any of that, because he was flat out working on the three Cat Life Centres. As he told Chloe during one of their calls, 'I've had my ring hanging out.'

'Charming image,' she'd laughed. He'd laughed, too, thrilled at the easy pace and warmth of their relationship. The vast distance between them was really helping.

At the end of the second week, which had been frenetic and fatiguing, Rex wanted to order a pizza, demolish his six-pack of powerful pale ales, and maybe watch a little porn. His shack was a haven, and he didn't let anyone in. The only people he spoke to while he was in there were himself and Chloe, and even she had been noticeably absent in the last few days. He hoped she was okay but didn't dare call her; she tended not to take surprises like that very well.

He was just opening his second stubby and perusing the porn options available on his computer – the only thing out-numbering cat videos on the internet is porn videos – when there was a light tap on his door. Peeved and ready to bite the head off the knocker, he got up and made sure his pants were buttoned, then opened the door. Sebastian stood there looking nervous but resolute. Nobody wanted to disturb Rex when he was having his alone time – who knew what they would chance upon?

'House meeting, Rex,' said Sebastian, the timidity in his voice reflected in his cowering stance, as though he would jump up, spin around and run away if Rex should lash out at him or even so much as utter one harsh word.

'Fuck.'

That Rex said this in a general sense rather than straight at him relaxed Sebastian a bit.

'Yeah, I know, right,' he said. 'Casper says no opt-outs.'

'Fuck.' Throwing back the entire contents of his near full stubby and cracking a fresh one to take with him, Rex followed Sebastian up to the big house. A scatter of rain smattered the path and dusted the pool with tiny dimples.

The entire household was gathered around the huge informal dining table adjoining the commercial kitchen, and the mood was sober. Casper looked to be seething in a silent, steaming kind of way, while Paris looked annoyed and put out, and the girls and boys were all quiet. Gazes were averted and conversation non-existent, and Skye's eyes were red-rimmed. There was a glowing pink mark on her arm, as though she had been grabbed hard.

As soon as Sebastian and Rex were seated, Casper stood up. His countenance was formidable, and for the first time in memory he was wearing dark colours – a black skivvy with a roll-neck that made him seem like a powerful overlord or a Bond villain.

'I'm a tolerant man,' he said. No one had the temerity to disagree. 'I've made all this happen. I built our church and I built our membership through sheer hard work and the magic of truth. I pay thousands of dollars a week rent on this place. I feed and entertain you all, and I employ you all in various capacities. So you could say that as well as a tolerant man, I am a generous one. Agreed?' Vigorous nodding of heads and a chorus of *yeses* and *absolutelys*.

'But for some people, that's not enough.'

He walked around the table and stood behind Skye, laying his hands heavily on her shoulders. She looked petrified. 'Skye has a confession to make. Don't you, Skye?'

Frightened, reluctant to speak but unable to defy the man standing over her, Skye nodded. 'Well, go on,' he prodded.

'My mum thinks you're … my mum doesn't believe in Felinism and she thinks this is a cult.'

'What?' His voice had a depth and menace none of them had heard before. Well, except maybe Paris, who, acting as though this was nothing new to her, stared off into the distance, waiting for this trial to end.

'My mum doesn't believe in Felinism,' Skye repeated.

'So. Your mum doesn't believe in Felinism. Well, we may as well all pack up and go home, because your mum is now the arbiter of all that's good and true. My years of building a philosophy, a teaching, of creating a positive influence on the lives of hundreds of thousands of believers, and of travelling the world sharing my truth, were a complete waste of time. Because Mrs Skye's-fucking-mum says it's not true. You know what, Skye? I don't believe your mum. I think she's wrong. I think she's trying to destroy your life and mine and everyone else's, because she's jealous. Because she wants you at home, tied to her apron strings and being the baby she never wanted to let go. She denies an undeniable truth, because she wants her little Skye at her beck and call.'

Casper's voice had been rising throughout this tirade, and he had begun to approach the vein-bulging stage.

'But truth doesn't die because some suburban cunt with an axe to grind says it should. Truth has its own life, and it's up to you to choose whether you'll follow that truth – follow me – or go running home back to Mummy. So what's it going to be?' he roared.

Skye sat quaking and didn't answer. Casper resumed in a much quieter voice. 'I thought so. And I wish that could be the end of it, I really do. But Skye's mum, the fucking oracle, said something that I want to address here and now, and for good. Because it's something that hurts me deeply, and which I never want to hear again in this house. Tell us, Skye.'

Skye cringed as Casper stood behind her, terror written all over her face and trembling body. She said nothing.

'Come on. Out with it. The other thing you told me.' His command was palpable, and Skye was unable to even consider resisting, though the pain it cost her to say it was unmistakable.

'She says you're a Svengali.'

'A Svengali!' Casper boomed. 'A man who seduces and manipulates poor, innocent young folk like you for his own nefarious purposes. A charlatan. A hustler and a thief. A user. Does this sound like a description of me to you?'

Another chorus, this time of *noes* and *absolutely nots*.

'I've tried to be nice. I've given you all everything I have, and I've brought you all into my inner circle. I've told you the deepest truth a human can know, and I've showed you the future we all share because of my hard work, my revelations and my understanding.'

As he spoke, Casper stalked slowly around the table, looking at each one of them in turn. None could look away. His gaze was a magnet, a fire that must be stared into until the eyes water and the brain submits. He returned to his own spot at the head of the table.

'And all I ask in return is a little respect!' He smacked an open hand on the thick mahogany table, and the thumping slap echoed around the room. Rex's beer did a little jump and almost fell over. 'A little loyalty. A little belief and support. Is that too much to ask?' A reprise of the most recent chorus ricocheted around the table.

'Your mother,' he said, boring a hole into Skye's face with those piercing, pickaxe eyes of his, 'is a cunt. She's a cunt. What is she, Paris?'

'She's a cunt.'

'Coco?'

'She's a cunt.'

'Yuki?' And so on around the table, so that everyone – some more or less hesitant than the others – laid the epithet on Skye's mother. Rex was distressed by having to say it, but he understood that his future with the organisation, and this exciting, cushy and now well-paid life, depended on it. At last, Skye was the only one left. She was beaten. Floored and flattened by the process. All the life had gone out of her body and all the blood had gone from her face. She was as pale and shapeless as a flour bag. 'Skye?'

'She's a cunt.'

'Who's a cunt?'

'My mother.'

'So say it. Say, "My mother is a cunt." '

'My mother is a cunt.' The tears were flowing freely now. Everyone else tried to find an item of interest on the wall opposite them.

Casper grinned, a jubilant, malicious sneer that distorted his beautiful face and made it hideous.

'Yuki, take her phone.' Yuki, sitting next to Skye, turned to comply, and Skye handed it over, her tear-wet face expressionless. 'You are not to see, talk to, communicate with or send messages of any kind to that woman ever again,' Casper commanded. 'Cut the cunt off. Paris, what should she do?'

'Cut the cunt off.'

'Coco?'

'Cut the cunt off.'

And so ensued another round of dutiful repetition, with less uncertainty than before – the group had found a unifying energy in submission.

'You're confined to the house for the next two weeks. No outside contact at all, no outings, no nothing. You'll study Felinism. You'll read everything I've ever written on the subject, and you'll commit your life to our beliefs. If I hear so much as a squeak of denial or a hint of disbelief, your next trick will be to take a swan dive off the Gap. Understand?'

Skye nodded miserably, and Izzy, on her other side, leaned over and gave her a hug, whispering gentle encouragement.

'The good news is, over the next few weeks, you and I will be spending a lot of quality time together,' Casper said as his eyebrows twitched suggestively. 'I'll make sure you forget all about that interfering old bitch,' he added in a more gentle, conciliatory tone.

Shrugging off his fury like a cloak, Casper opened his arms out and smiled broadly. He was beautiful again. 'Okay everyone,' he said with that natural merriment that made him so irresistible, 'have a great Friday night.'

29. Cats are lavish

When a cat likes you, or has discovered a need for your services and wishes to encourage your allegiance, they can be extravagant in their affections and favours. A pigeon liver left on the doorstep is a token of their highest esteem. You will feel like the only and luckiest being in the world, because you are the recipient not just of their largesse, but their attentions. When you can arouse such grateful responses in others, you will be more like a cat.

Casper

Back in his comfy cabana, Rex didn't finish his six-pack or order a pizza. Shaken, he sat for a while in the dark, feeling sick about Skye and wondering just how oppressive and dictatorial Casper could get. Sure, he'd seen the Cat Man chuck some impressive paddies before, but this was a whole new level of savagery. He understood that what Skye's mum had said could be damaging to the group if left unaddressed, because it could poison the collective mind by implying that Casper had some motive other than evangelising Felinism. But did he have to be so brutal? So visceral? So straight-out threatening?

He went to bed early, thinking he was just a simple chippy who had no real idea of how to create and sustain a massive enterprise like the Church of Felinism. Maybe its higher purpose did demand a certain hard-hearted resolve, and maybe harsh medicine was required at times. Still, he wished he hadn't taken part in that scene. How it would colour his relationship with Casper remained to be seen.

Saturday morning was diamond-bright and clear, and as the sun crested the horizon across the harbour, Rex was scooping the leaves out of the pool. It wasn't one of his prescribed jobs, but he often spent the first part of the day out there, looking with wistful enjoyment across the serenity of the bay, engaging his hands and body in the pleasurably mindless pursuit of removing foreign bodies from the clean, chlorinated water.

He was reluctant to go up to breakfast, but couldn't put it off forever, so he went into his cabin, showered and put on some work gear. The workers wouldn't be on-site on a Saturday, but that would give him an opportunity to inspect the quality of the work done at all three locations in peace and quiet, and maybe spend some time measuring, cutting and doing other prep work for Monday. It would keep him out of the mansion and Casper's sights, and that would suit him fine. If there was a need for any security stuff, he could hopefully delegate it to Mick or Gus, and if Casper insisted that Rex do it, he could be back and changed into his suit without too much trouble.

Breakfast was weirdly normal. There was no sign of Skye, as expected, and Casper and Paris were absent as usual, but the rest of the crew were their usual chatty, catty selves with just a teeny undertone of enforced exuberance. Nobody talked about the previous night or mentioned Skye, except when

Yuki suggested that she might take something up to 'poor Skye.' Rex was glad he had the distraction of work, so he ate and excused himself.

He'd parked the hired van he used for work a little way down the street, so he exited the gates of the Cat House and felt the weight of the last twelve hours lift off him. He'd always found work fulfilling, so a quiet day alone on-site was just what he needed.

His newfound optimism disappeared faster than a bastard on Father's Day when he realised that where the van had been the night before, there was now a shiny four-wheel-drive ute kitted out with every knick-knack you could fit on such a vehicle. He was surprised not to see a satellite dish. Some rich local wanker, no doubt. So, his hire van had been pinched, with all his tools, his drawings and everything else in it.

Fuck! Casper would be spewing. This wasn't the kind of news the boss needed right now, and Rex was definitely not keen to be the one to deliver it, or to receive the ear bashing that would be the reaction. Casper would rant on about how careless Rex must have been, how it would be up to him to make good with the hire company and insurers, how he felt like he should be out there holding Rex's fucking hand every step of the way, and why couldn't people be as smart and as careful and as effective as he was, and so on and so on. It was sure to be torture. He hung his head and turned to go back to face the music, lifting his leaden feet with slow and methodical determination, one after the other.

A couple of paces along, he looked up and found Casper standing at the gates of the house, watching him with playful, catlike curiosity. Shit. He wouldn't even have time to prepare a story. Not that it would do any good. He figured if he was lucky, he'd end up in the doghouse for a few days. If not, he'd be going home. Still, that would be something.

'The van...' he began.

'Gone, eh?' said Casper.

'I locked it, man. I swear. I just...'

Casper said nothing. He raised his arm and pointed it down the street, pressing a button on the gadget in his hand. *Fweet fweet*, went the wanky four-wheel drive, and Rex almost snapped his neck turning around to see what the sound was. His eye fell on the vehicle just as the indicator light flashed to signal that it was unlocked. Swivelling his head again, he turned to look at Casper. The Cat Man was grinning at him, showing his pearl-white teeth and that tiny, pink sliver of gum that signified actual sincerity. He walked over to where Rex stood rooted to the spot, and dropped the keys in his hands.

'It's yours, mate,' he said.

Rex was in shock. What? What did this mean? Could it be real?

'Go on,' said Casper. 'Take a closer look at your new ride.'

Speechless, Rex ran over to the kerb and drank in the sight of that magnificent vehicle. Brand spanking new, with all the fruit – roof rack, lock-up toolbox, bull bar with dual halogen spotlights, jet black duco and chrome mags. There was even a personalised number plate – Dog Boy. It was a thing of rare beauty and power, like a race-winning greyhound, only better.

'What the f—?' Rex spluttered at last. He couldn't even get his favourite expletive out.

Casper was opening the passenger door, showing him the inside, which was as plush as any limo they'd ever shared, but with a better stereo system.

'I haven't forgotten how you backed me up over that Tilly shit,' said Casper. 'And I wanted to show you how much I appreciate everything you're doing. You know, you're an important part of the church now. And I know you'll keep on supporting me, even when I have to take tough measures.'

Rex tried to speak, but he had nothing. He stared at the car, at Casper, back at the car and back again at his benefactor, his mouth open. Casper gave a little laugh of joy and ownership, and got into the passenger seat.

'Go on, get in,' he said.

Rex circled around and got into the driver's seat. It was like a jet cockpit, with dials and displays all over the shop, a huge GPS screen in the centre of the dash, and to top it off, a bobble-head model of Bastet sitting on the dashboard. He gripped the steering wheel and imagined himself driving the beast. He looked at his boss again, as if to see if this was really real.

'It's all yours, mate,' said Casper with a wink. 'All paid for, juiced up and ready to go. I think the papers are in the console. Why don't you have a look?'

Rex opened the console and peered inside, but instead of a registration document, there was a square blue box. On the top, it said Rolex.

'Shit, how did that get there?' said Casper with an impish grin. 'Better grab it.'

Rex followed orders, pulling the box out. He opened it up and inside was a Yacht-Master watch with a smart grey dial and gleaming stainless-steel band. If he hadn't been sitting in the most gorgeous automotive creation on the planet, Rex would have sworn it was the most beautiful thing he'd ever seen.

'Put it on,' said Casper.

Rex couldn't get his scabby old G-Shock off fast enough, and slipped the heavy jewel over his wrist. It fit perfectly. He looked up at Casper, his eyes wide and his mouth hanging open like a broken backyard dunny door. 'Fuck,' he said. 'I just … I can't … fuck.'

The Cat Man cackled and patted him on the shoulder.

'Bro,' he said. 'You really are like a brother to me. Having you behind me gives me confidence and strength. Besides,' he lightened up, 'you've been working your arse off, and those fucking hire vans are ugly and shit to drive. I just wanted to give you a hand.'

'What can I say?' said Rex. It was all he could do to quell the tears welling up in his eyes. 'I can't believe it; this is just fantastic. Thank you. Thank you. Thank you.'

Chuckling, Casper pulled his seat belt across his torso and clicked it into place. 'You deserve it. And you'll find a full set of new tools in the back. Nothing but the best for my mate.'

'Shit,' was all Rex could manage.

'Now, give us a lift down to Alexandria, over near the airport, would you? I need to pick up my new Rolls.'

30. Cats are mercurial

Being more like a cat means giving in to your feelings all the way, all the time. If that means you move from hysteria to smug complacency in less time than it takes a normal person to button a shirt, so be it. It keeps people guessing, and it makes it seem like you're in touch with your emotions. Be more like a cat.

Casper

Casper was having a tantrum. A full-on, smash things up, tear things down and wail 'why does everything happen to me?' hissy fit of epic proportions. He was literally crying and there was some solid gnashing of teeth going on; it was unmanly and even inhuman.

Mind you, he had something of a good reason to be peeved. Butch McNab, that dreary little journalist with the face of a junkyard dog and the attitude of its mother, had penned a terrible smear piece about him, and the *Sun-Herald*, the Sunday paper, had seen fit to print it.

'Look at this!' Casper wailed. 'This is what that little fucker has written about me: "Australian Casper White may no longer be able to return to the United States following revelations that he fled the country to avoid facing an impending Internal Revenue Service probe into his 'church,' the cult of Felinism, which has now spread to his home country. This reporter has seen documents that suggest that the tax-free status of the cult in the United States is under review. Should that status be revoked, the church itself and its charismatic founder could be liable for many millions in retrospective taxes and penalties. Rumours abound that White is a charlatan who uses his mysterious connection with the cats that fill his Cat Life Centres – really just glorified cat cafes – to seduce many of his mainly female followers, as well as to extract millions in ongoing payments to the church from wealthy supporters. Mr White fritters away this money on first-class travel, luxury homes and vehicles, expensive gifts for his growing entourage, and endless quantities of proverbial wine, women and song." '

He threw the newspaper across the room and stalked around looking for something or someone to smash.

Paris picked up the crumpled newspaper and continued reading aloud. The article ended by insinuating that the upper levels of church membership involved buying into some bizarre beliefs that it was rumoured involved aliens. She scoffed as she read that last paragraph, adding, 'At least you already dealt with that in your 60 Minutes interview.'

Still, the Cat Man was unimpressed – to the point of being homicidal.

'God damn that shitty little motherfucker,' he blustered as he threw an expensive vase at an even more overpriced mirror. 'Fuck him and his whole fucking family. I'll go after them all and tear them to shreds! I'll feed them to the worms and shit on their bones. Why would that fucking spineless turd do this

to me? What have I done to him? Oh, he'll get his. That fucker.'
And much more in the same vein – a cyclical stream of curses,
cries of victimhood and promises to get even in the most
uneven ways possible.

The inevitable media follow-up kicked in even as the
shards of glass and splinters of timber were still being
showered around the room. The phones started ringing, the
emails poured in, and Paris and Oscar were besieged. Paris
had to break off from deflecting the media to talk Casper
off his metaphorical ledge and try to formulate some kind of
positive spin on the mess.

Rex was party to much of this, having been enlisted by
Paris to help calm the boss down, without any real success.
Eventually she gave up and bailed out, leaving Casper to his
histrionics.

'Spoiled little shit,' she said to Rex as she left the room.
Rex just stood there, mouth slightly agape and mind bending
around the self-centred babble Casper was continuing to spew
and sputter, wondering again just what this man might be
capable of perpetrating, given the right motivation.

As Paris walked away, Casper shouted that he wouldn't
talk to the media. Indeed, he didn't talk to anyone for a whole
day, but sat in his room sulking. Paris officially denied the
whole thing and derided Butch McNab as a washed-up hack,
a failed cop and an obnoxious little terrier who just needed
to be thrown a bone. She wrote about the Australian habit of
'cutting down tall poppies,' accused McNab of being jealous
and ignorant of the church's true message and dismissed his
US sources as being uninformed. She used the term 'fake news'
repeatedly to excellent effect, and made Casper seem like the
hapless prey of an unwarranted attack.

The story didn't go much further, mainly because Butch McNab could not produce even copies of the documents he had referred to, and because too many people had seen the *60 Minutes* piece. The overwhelming public view was that Casper was a lovely and honest person who just happened to run a weird cult. The most interesting – and vigorous – response came from the Felinist community.

Believers, feliphiles and Casper lovers came out in droves to defend him and his organisation, and they hounded Butch McNab across every social media outlet they could find, labelling him a liar, a muckraker and a fake-news artist, along with many less polite expressions. He was lambasted, parodied, maligned and shamed, and warned in no uncertain terms to leave Casper alone lest he face the wrath of a host of supporters with bared teeth and sharpened claws.

The next day, Casper decided he needed a break, so he and Rex jumped in Rex's sexy new ute and struck out for the coast south of Sydney. They spent a couple of days in cold, wet and windy Huskisson on the shores of Jervis Bay, sitting inside a bar by a fire and talking quietly. No one in the town recognised Casper, or cared who he was enough to interrupt him if they did, and he was quickly refreshed.

By the end of the first afternoon, a good few schooners in, he was more fascinating and appealing than ever before, and even more friendly to Rex. He stepped up the indoctrination, regaling Rex with tales of the early days of the Great Experiment, and drew him into elaborate speculations as to the idyllic future that awaited them on Meon. At times he was quite emotional, and seemed to Rex to be a vulnerable, misunderstood and genuine soul who just needed to be loved.

A few beers later, Casper was even willing to admit that

his whole catechism could seem less than credible to the objective observer.

'I know people can pick my history of the relationship between cats and humans apart if they try hard enough,' he said. 'But scientists don't know with any certainty that cats didn't come from space, or that previous generations of cats didn't have the ability to communicate more directly and articulately to the minds of the humans of the time, who were much less developed and sophisticated than we are. And in any case, it doesn't matter. As religions have shown time and time again across the centuries, belief is a choice. As long as the story is even vaguely plausible – and mine is at least as likely as many others – people will be happy to believe it. They want to believe in something, and they're willing to over-look certain inconsistencies if the belief you're giving them is uplifting and joyful and provides hope.

'Now, it just so happens that I am telling the rock-solid truth, so people – even smart, cynical types like you – can see that. You understand that I'm being honest with you, and you value the truth. You're not just in it for the space travel, like so many others.'

Rex felt privileged to see this raw, honest side of Casper, and he had no doubt that the Cat Man was genuine and secure in his faith. Their time together further cemented Rex's belief in Felinism, its leader and its origins.

It was a delightful interlude and a great bonding opportunity, not to mention a welcome respite for the tight-knit team left shacked up in Potts Point, terrified of what the next outburst might bring. When the lads came home late on the third day with cheery grins and satisfying stubble growth, the others in the Cat House breathed a collective sigh of relief.

31. Cats are vulnerable

They may be tough, independent and resilient, but cats are not invincible. Sometimes events conspire to hurt, upset or disorient them. When that happens, a clever cat has no compunction in seeking the sympathy and assistance of others. Be more like a cat.

Casper

Head back, eyes closed and mouth ever so slightly open, as natural as Rex had ever seen him, Casper had slept in the passenger seat on the drive back to Sydney. Looking at him, Rex was confused about Casper, their association and Felinism.

On the one hand, he'd found many, many reasons to like the boss, and had at times found him to be warm, trusting, smart, funny, believable and even cuddly. And that was not even to mention the generosity he'd showered, not just on Rex but on all the members of the entourage, especially in the aftermath of the Skye incident.

On the other hand, there was now a broad catalogue of disturbing episodes involving Casper, and aspects of his personality could be terrifying, troubling or grating – from his autocratic approach to his wildfire temper, selfish egoism and childish resentments.

But over the couple of days they'd spent together down in Huskisson, many of Casper's better qualities had come out, and none of the bad. That had strengthened Rex's positive feelings for the Cat Man and his church, which was good, because he wanted to feel positive about them. Felinism was fast becoming second nature to him, and he found himself daydreaming about the day when the cats would come back and whisk him off to Meon with all the other true believers. It was a stirring idea, and a powerful incentive to keep on believing and building the church.

He also felt that part of his value to the organisation was his ability to exert a moderating influence on Casper, by his sheer size if not his capacity to reason with the boss. He didn't want to let the upsetting experiences outweigh the good, so he resolved, on that drive back, to keep a weather eye on Casper, but to remain optimistic.

Things had settled down a lot when they returned, which helped. Rex had a bit of catching up to do on his multiple construction projects, so he was busy and loving it, and Casper was back to being his usual serene, perceptive and personable self with the crew – with the obvious exception of Paris, who he drove like a horse.

Skye had been given the freedom of the house but was not allowed to leave and banned from any electronics, but she was accepting of her situation and grateful to still be there. It was clear from the way she looked at him and obeyed him that she still adored Casper and was prepared to take his word that her mother was the one at fault. For his part, the boss spent a lot of time with Skye, counselling her in that special way of his, which produced screams of delight that could be heard in every corner of the house. In between those physical ministrations, he indoctrinated her against her mother, her family and all of her friends. Needless to say, it worked.

So for a short, blissful while, all was as it should have been. The only tiny fly in this soothing ointment was Chloe. She had gone dark on Rex, and he didn't know why. Sure, he sometimes got a little short when she quizzed him endlessly about Casper's days and nights, his speeches, his hair, his clothes, his assignations and even his bloody diet. But most of the time he put up with it, lapping up her attention like it was a bowl of his favourite beer. Now, though, there had been no word for a week or more, and he was worried about her.

On the fourth of July, Coco and Yuki, being good American girls, organised a day of celebrations culminating in a house barbecue as the sun set exquisitely over the vast harbour. It was cool but not winter-cold, the first clear day for almost a week, and the evening was spectacular. All the second-tier members of the household had been partying since their early lunch, and were in boisterous good form when Rex arrived home after another long day at work. He had no energy for a boozy session with the crew, but they were right outside his pool house making a hell of a racket, and in any case, they were as usual not taking no for an answer.

He joined the party, cracking a beer and standing by the barbie, spinning the snaggers and flipping the steaks more than was strictly required. He was an old-fashioned Aussie flesh-turner in that regard, firm in his belief that cooking on a barbecue demands the constant examination and rerrange-ment of the fat and gristle being charred.

He was just starting to get into the swing of things,

having necked sufficient stubbies to unlock his goofy fun side, when his phone buzzed in his pocket. Chloe! At last. He darted into his shanty and pressed the button.

'G'day,' he said with what he believed to be cheerful charm.

'Oh, Rex,' Chloe sobbed. 'Thank god.'

It was though the cold hand of death had reached into Rex's chest and clapped its bony fingers around his heart. A chill swept through him, and he ached with every fibre to be there with Chloe, nuzzling into her neck and lending her his warmth and strength.

'Chloe.' It was a cry of despair at the distance between them. 'What's happened?'

'It's too awful. You'll think I'm awful. I don't know what to do. It's not fair.'

'Tell me. I'd never think you're awful, you know that.' He was trying to keep calm for her sake, but the only thing out-pacing the thoughts running pell-mell through his mind was his pulse. He sat down on his grubby two-seat couch. 'Now, what's wrong?'

'It's all ruined, that's what. Everything. My job, my life, any relationship I might have had with Casper.' Nice stab, that one. Got him right in the jugular.

'Okay, just calm down and tell me exactly what's happened.'

'I'm pregnant.'

Knife removed from throat, reinserted into brain. The racing thoughts stopped and were replaced by a buzzing stillness, a kind of tinnitus of the soul. Pregnant? Jesus. And then the tumult of emotions: confusion, dismay, anger, jealousy, terror, love, hate, happiness and ineffable sadness. If all that was happening to him, what was Chloe feeling? Holy shit. He tried to get it together, to be the strong presence she obviously needed at that moment.

'I see,' he said, his voice leaden gravel.

'And I don't care what happens, I'm having it.' Her voice was sullen, defiant, tremulous, as though she expected to be alone in all the tribulations her courageous decision would incur but held onto a sliver of hope that maybe she wouldn't need to be. And then a bolt of pure white light exploded in Rex's brain, an eruption of delicious possibility that sent a fountain of serotonin flooding through his every synapse. The rush vanished as quickly as it had come on. He knew the answer, but had to ask. After all, less than two weeks before Casper had come to Australia and jumped her, Chloe had thrown him that wonderful bone.

'Could it be … mine?'

The crushing exasperation in her tone reminded him of why he should have thought it through a bit longer before giving voice to that stupid, irrational dream.

'Oh, fuck off, Rex. For Christ's sake, that's all I need, is to be having your fucking pups. We both know this is Casper's baby. You know what, forget it. Forget I ever called. I don't know why I thought for a second I would ever get any sense out of you, let alone any help.'

Even a dog will only take so much of a kicking before it creeps off to lick its wounds, and that was one hell of a kicking. Rex was angry with himself for thinking that that there was even a remote chance that the baby could be his, but even angrier with her for taking the suggestion in such high dudgeon. Would it honestly be so awful if he was the baby's father? The only thing that mattered was that Chloe thought so.

Just as suddenly as that mad thought had arisen, all his remaining optimism for their relationship crashed to the ground.

'Of course,' he said stiffly and with surprising dignity. 'How stupid of me. Good luck.' And he hung up. It killed him to do it, but he didn't know what else to do. Maybe he'd get over her eventually. Maybe he'd settle for another one of Casper's cast-offs – some dumb, beautiful but inoffensive girl who wouldn't mind spending a life being spoiled and eventually maybe even adored.

His phone rang again. He didn't want to answer it – he wasn't ready for more abuse right then – but he couldn't ignore it. It was Chloe, after all.

'Hello?' His greeting was tentative, inquiring. She was in tears.

'I'm so sorry, Rexy,' she blubbered. 'You've always been so good to me and I'm such a bitch, but I can't help it. You know I care about you, don't you?'

Not knowing how to respond, Rex said nothing. The words *I care about you* were still bouncing around in his brain, and the honesty with which they had been delivered had already made up for everything else.

'Rexy? Don't be mad.'

'I'm not mad. I'm worried about you. I want to help.'

'Then tell me what I should do. Should I tell Casper? What do you think he'll do?'

'If he's a man, he'll stand by you. I would.'

'I know you would. You're such an awesome friend. I really am sorry about the way I reacted, it's just that I'm confused and nervous and scared, and I need you on my side. Asking if it could be yours just made the whole thing seem so much more complicated and messy, and made me feel like such a slut.'

'You're not. You're not a slut; you're an incredible, warm, loving person. I am so sorry I said that, I really am. I know it was stupid.'

She chuckled softly and a little sadly. 'In some ways, it would be much better if it was yours.'

He couldn't speak, because he couldn't trust his voice not to break.

'But it is what it is, Rexy,' she continued, her tone brisker and more businesslike. 'I guess I just have to deal with it. I'll call him tomorrow.'

'Whatever happens, you know I'll support you.'

'I know that, darling, and I love you for it. But this is my battle, and I'll fight it my way. I've got to go, Rexy; thank you for talking to me.'

And she was gone. But she'd said she cared, she'd used the L word, for god's sake, and she'd even acknowledged his past service. He sat holding his phone for a long time, then finally put it down to pick up his beer. He had a long slurp, put it down on the table and stared into the dark nothingness for a while. He couldn't go back out to the party, which was sounding pretty wild by then. He knew they wouldn't miss him, anyway. He sat in the dark and polished off the remainder of his six-pack, then went to bed.

32. Dogs chase their own tails

Dogs are easily confused, and have been known to waste hours at a time chasing their own tails. They're big softies who think with their hearts and lead with their chins, and they never get what they really want because they don't know what that is. Don't be a dog; be a cat.

Casper

The Bondi Cat Life Centre was coming along very well. Rex had a team of builders and carpenters working on the fit-out, and it was all coming together tickety-boo. But he couldn't keep his mind on the job, because he was thinking about Chloe. He walked off the site and took a long ramble along the busy Bondi beachfront. Even on this crisp winter's day there was plenty of action along the bay. Surfers scrambled for head-high crumbling waves, seagulls squabbled over dropped chips and tossed scraps, and tourists from every part of the world snapped selfies with the famous strand stretching out behind them.

The problem before Rex was complex. How would he handle seeing Casper and Chloe together every day? Would he be able to keep on working for the church and coming into contact with the lost love of his life every day? Could he bear to be near her, to watch Casper touching her, kissing her, maybe being cruel and ignoring her the way he did to others? How would he take it? Would he be moved to kill his boss? That wouldn't look good on his resume. Would he cry himself to sleep every night, knowing she was so near and yet so far away? What if, while he was with him, Casper did things Rex knew would upset Chloe if she found out, and the boss demanded his loyal silence? He just didn't know if he could take it.

There was no question in his mind that Casper would jump at the chance to make Chloe his wife. He'd be a bloody fool not to. If Rex was in Casper's shoes, he'd be out scouting mid-priced rings right now. No, if he was in Casper's flashy footwear, he'd be out searching for the biggest, finest fuck-off diamond he could find. No expense spared. And planning the wedding of the century.

He could see, in his mind, the media spectacular to be made out of the marriage of Casper and Chloe. She would be ethereal, lovely, with just the slenderest baby bump visible beneath a white rushing river of flowing silk and tulle, and Casper would be wearing the whitest, tightest and most fashionable tux ever seen, possibly – in Rex's imagination – with a white top hat tilted at a rakish angle on his gilded head. It would be beautiful beyond belief.

The trouble was, he couldn't even see himself in the picture. He guessed he'd be out standing by the car, holding the fucking door open. That would be right; he'd be their faithful doormat for the rest of his days, pouring his life into theirs and gaining no reward or recognition for it, just endless years of pain and servitude. He'd probably even just take it in silence when later, because he couldn't keep it in his pants for five minutes, Casper announced that the Church of Felinism supports polygamy, and started building a harem of stunning yet submissive wives.

Yes, he thought, he would have to move on. But then it occurred to him that if he did, he'd never see Chloe, Casper or this exhilarating, unpredictable and lucrative life again. It was bad enough to be losing Chloe, but there was also the thorny issue of the Cat Man and Felinism itself. Casper had been his friend; his mentor, master and idol, especially lately. They'd shared some dazzling successes, and when Casper reached a low ebb, as sometimes happens to a person who's under the sort of pressure he was, he confided in Rex. He was always earnest in his gratitude, and often complimented Rex on the quality and value of his advice.

He was one of the first people ever to make Rex feel appreciated and held in high regard, and he treasured that feeling and the man who had given it to him. He didn't want to bail out and let the boss down, but he wasn't sure he wanted to hang around and watch the Casper and Chloe fairy tale unfold in rich happiness while he lurked, invisible, in the shadows. Then again, if it all went to shit, if he was still on hand, he'd be there to pick up the pieces and help Chloe through the toughest time of her life. That might be worth something.

Casper had shown himself to be harsh, indifferent, diabolically demanding and sometimes ruthless to the people around him, but he'd never been too far out of line with Rex, and it was difficult to believe that he wouldn't treat Chloe with respect. Surely, as his wife she would merit special consideration. And if not, Rex would have been a fucking idiot to walk away right when she needed him most.

Above all, would it be right to reject the friendship the

Cat Man offered – and all the bonuses that went with it – on the basis of a few incidents that he'd witnessed but not otherwise been affected by, or the possibility that he might not treat Chloe as she deserved? Rex didn't think so.

There had been times lately when he had been captivated by Casper and had wanted fervently to believe everything about Felinism. It was an enchanting and dizzying prospect, to be transported across the galaxy to a faraway planet inhabited by a race of super cats who could speak to him with their minds and show him thoughts and ideas that surpassed anything anyone on earth has ever seen. With his construction skills, Rex fancied he would be the cats' champion builder, creating amazing, outlandish and eternal edifices that would etch his name in intergalactic history.

It was tough to know what to do. If he listened to his head, he would stay, keep an eye on them both, maybe enjoy their success and profit from it, maybe spend his life in shadowy misery, and just maybe swoop in and save Chloe from an unhappy marriage. Whatever happened, if he stayed, he would become an important member of the church, and one day, with luck sooner rather than later, he would become the master builder of Meon, a legend throughout the cosmos.

The trouble was that in his heart, Rex really wanted to be on the next jet to Perth to propose to Chloe before Casper had the chance, and to hell with the consequences. The only thing that stopped him was the thought of the look of horror on Chloe's face when he got down on one knee and produced a cubic-zirconia ring.

He turned back towards the worksite, baffled about what to do and feeling guilty about all the competing emotions within him. There was nothing for it but to see what happened next.

33. Cats are psychopaths

A cat in a towering rage is terrifying to behold, and the ensuing self-pity party can be pathetic, but when it's time to get down to business, their fury will be replaced by heartless brutality and pitiless efficiency, delivered with glacial composure. It may seem cold, but ruthlessness breeds respect and admiration. Be more like a cat – lose your scruples.

Casper

'Did you know about this?' Casper was sitting behind the desk in his private office, a lavish retreat in mahogany and leather overlooking the bay. The wide, lacquered desk held a genuine, life-sized Egyptian statue of Bastet, a signed photo of Casper with Stubbs – the feline mayor of Talkeetna in Alaska – a solid gold mouse, and an original cel from a Felix the Cat cartoon. Behind Casper, there was a large portrait of him holding Tardar Sauce, famous throughout the world as 'Grumpy Cat,' the cat's glum scowl contrasting with the Cat Man's beatific smile.

The real Casper was not smiling. His polar-blue eyes seemed to be throwing icy daggers at Rex, who had his hands behind his back and his head bowed in submission. He knew exactly what the boss was referring to, but instinct told him to play dumb. Like the puppy confronted with the chewed shoe or the sloppy turd spread out on the carpet, he affected both innocence and ignorance at the same time.

Casper wasn't buying it. 'Come on, did you know or not?'

He had to follow through now. 'About what?'

'About fucking Chloe, of course. About her plan to trap me with a fucking baby. Are you in on it? Is this some kind of shakedown? Because you'll get nothing. Less than nothing.'

Rex said, 'She rang me last night and told me she was pregnant. That's all I know.' He stared at the carpet as he said this, not seeing just how much his disinclination to face Casper further inflamed him.

Casper managed to moderate his voice, speaking in a low growl. 'Look at me, Rex. Look at me. Are you sure that's all you know?'

Rex met the gaze, managed not to flinch. 'I'm positive. She called me in tears, and that's the first I've heard of it.'

'So why didn't you tell me straight away?'

'It was late. You were with the girls. It wasn't my place. This is between you and Chloe.'

The last bit lit another fuse behind Casper's eyes. 'What the fuck does that mean? What are you two up to?'

'Honestly, nothing. How could I say something? How could I be involved in anything?'

'Well, that's true. You're so fucking pathetic she'd be a bloody idiot to tell you anything. I'm surprised she even told you that much.'

Rex winced at the description of him but stayed quiet; he was on a hiding to nothing in this argument.

There was a sudden change in Casper's demeanour. No longer accusing, he morphed into the lamenting victim, dropping his head into his hands and adopting a whimpering tone. 'She's betrayed me, Rex,' he moaned. 'Why would she do that? Haven't I been good to her? Didn't I give her everything?'

Rex stood as still as a statue. There was nothing he could add or reply, and to say the wrong thing might elicit another detonation.

There was more of the same for a short while, and then Casper straightened up. He licked the back of his wrist and rubbed it behind his ear, then put his hands straight out before him in a calming pose. 'She's out,' he said.

'What?' It escaped before Rex could rein it in.

'She's out. Gone. Out of the church, out of my life, gone.'

Rex sucked in his breath. Casper's eyes were drilling through his skull and into the soft, mushy part of his brain again. 'You got a problem with that?' The righteous anger was back, but it was a cold, determined intensity rather than a repeat of the earlier chaotic rage.

'Ummm...'

'Cause if you do, you're out too. In a fucking minute. Like right fucking now. But if I let you stay, whatever you call that shitty little connection you had with her – you'd never call it a relationship – that's over too. Finished. You know I need total loyalty, and now is the time to prove yours. You cut her off, Rex, or you're a goner. I never want to hear that bitch's name again. She betrayed me, she tried to trap me, and now she's gone. Understood?'

Rex was motionless, powerless to move because all the blood was rushing from his brain and his heart to his feet. He wasn't sure it wasn't leaking onto the floor beneath him. His face was pale, and his eyes were filming over with moisture.

He blinked.

'Don't fuck with me, Rex,' Casper said. His voice was commanding, his expression serious as dynamite. 'Just get the fuck out of here. And remember,' he said as Rex started to walk out. 'You'll never speak to her again, and her name will never be spoken again in my presence. Got it?'

Rex turned and nodded with slow, infinite sadness, then turned again kept and moving.

34. Dogs hate cats

There has always been a fundamental enmity between dogs and cats. Because dogs don't understand cats, and cats consider dogs weak, stupid animals that can be pushed around. The trouble comes when the dog has had enough and decides to bite back. If you're going to be like a cat, beware of the dog.

Casper

Rex kept on moving, out the door, down the path and along the road. He walked, unseeing, past the colonial magnificence of Elizabeth Bay House, and on into the grimy sleaze of Kings Cross. And with every step he took, every metre he made, he hated Casper more. He had at last seen his boss in his true colours and been on the receiving end of his merciless cruelty. He felt stupid.

Look at yourself, Rex, he said to himself. *Of course Casper was good to you. You're a big, meaty dog of a man who could rip him into little pussy shreds if you wanted to. He's afraid of your physical strength, even though he needs it. But while he was taking advantage of your muscle, he used and abused you men-*

tally. And all those times you let him get away with being a toxic bastard because you weren't the target, you were just being weak and selfish. You wanted to believe all that bullshit because it made you feel important and gave you hope about too many things. Get past it, man. Fucking grow a pair and go back and smack his fucking head in.

But he kept walking and talking to himself in censorious tones. He walked right into the heart of Kings Cross and found himself on the doorstep of the Empire Hotel. It wasn't yet lunchtime, but heading off on a stupendous bender presented itself as an excellent idea. Perhaps getting blind drunk would help him nut out a solution to his problem – how to escape from the Cat House, and from Casper and his church, in one piece.

He'd seen how savage Casper could be in not just refuting what he now saw as a strong argument from Skye's mother, but obliterating the authority of the one who'd suggested it and prohibiting any further contact with her. How would he take the defection of his security chief and construction supervisor? It would disrupt the building schedule, put the program out of whack and cost big bikkies to rectify, and Casper would lose his shit over that. But it was the betrayal, as the Cat Man perceived it, that would send him over the top. He'd chuck a huge dummy spit, look for ways to punish Rex, and cook up who knew what kind of revenge.

Rex ordered a drink and stared into space, wondering how the fuck he'd got himself into such a mess and how he'd get out. He worried about Chloe, fretted about his own safety and future, and grew ever more suspicious of what lengths Casper would go to keep him in the church. Or to keep him quiet if he insisted on leaving.

Several beers later, he was no closer to the answer, but felt less pained about it, and disinclined to go anywhere or do anything about it. Like a faint shadow that you become aware of on a cloudy day, a presence arrived by his side. It took a seat at the bar next to him, despite there being yards of empty bar space on either side. He turned to inspect the stealthy newcomer, expecting Paris, perhaps Coco or Yuki, or even Sebastian. It couldn't be Casper himself, could it? That would be beyond awkward.

Half expecting to be assaulted by whiteness, purity and arrogance, he was surprised to see a squat little man covered in rough bristles, wearing a crumpled shirt and a sleeveless puffer jacket, and wheezing as though the fifteen-metre walk from the door had just about killed him. The bloke looked vaguely familiar, but Rex couldn't place him. Though he wasn't big or bolshy enough to be a physical threat, the little fellow made him nervous.

How Butch came to find Rex at this critical juncture in his life, when he was contemplating grievous bodily harm to his former idol, is one of those mysteries that may never be solved. Maybe Butch had people keeping an eye out for Rex in the Cross, anticipating that just such a situation would one day arise. Perhaps he went to the Empire for lunch (three pints of lager and a packet of chips) every day. Or it was, perchance, providence? Fate? Coincidence?

In any case, Butch had no trouble recognising Rex, and even less reading the dismal expression on his face. He knew this hole would yield a bone – all he had to do was dig.

'G'day,' he said with an amiable grin.

35. Dogs dig things up

Dogs have an annoying habit of ferreting around where they're not wanted, of digging things up and leaving them out for everyone to see. They can't relax and leave well enough alone, they have to stick their noses into everything and make life difficult and tense. Why can't dogs just be more like cats?

Casper

Butch could smell the sadness and disappointment on Rex, but Rex was too self-absorbed and filled with loathing to catch the powerful scent of hyena emanating from the newcomer. He figured the nosy fellow next to him was nothing more than a local drunk turning up for his daily appointment with oblivion – the fellow had the unkempt appearance and slovenly slouch of one accustomed to slaughtering brain cells with great frequency. If only Rex had recognised that these are characteristics common to a great many journalists, and indeed to writers of all kinds.

'Looks like life's been chucking rocks at you, mate,' said Butch.

'Yeah, you could say that,' replied Rex. He was guarded, non-committal. He appreciated the company, but wasn't yet in the mood to talk.

'You know what fixes that? Shots.'

Rex turned to take a proper gander at the presence beside him. He was an ugly little fucker, with a smug, insider-knowledge air about his roly-poly frame and rosaceous face. Come to think of it, he'd definitely seen that pudgy mug before, hadn't he? He might have barred the bloke from some cat do or other, but what could that matter now, as long as he didn't hold a grudge? He looked harmless enough. And taking the short road to post-sobriety together wasn't a bad way to overcome any residual resentment the fellow might harbour.

'Tequila,' he said, and raised his beer glass, which the other clinked. Butch signalled the barman.

A round of shots went down, and Butch embarked on what appeared to be a spontaneous show of interest in the suffering of a fellow human but was in reality a long-planned inquisition. Like a dog with the remains of last night's lamb roast, he knew that one doesn't leap straight in and crack one's teeth in an impulsive attempt to get at the juicy marrow trapped inside. First you must lick and gnaw and worry the bone until it warms and softens, at which point it can be safely fractured with the gentle but sustained application of pressure.

'So, what's got you down, my friend?'

'Ah, just shit. Everything's shit,' said Rex.

'Well, I will agree with you on that score,' said Butch. 'But you know, if you talk about it, it can help. Who's the source of all this? Your boss? Your missus? Your bookie? Your dealer?'

This last at least elicited a snort of laughter from Rex, and a quick denial. 'Ha, shit no, not a dealer. I don't fuck with that shit. Nah, I suppose it's my boss. Or my former boss. I quit.'

Like a dachshund that's spotted a badger and is trying to work out the best way to follow it down its hole, Butch danced around the opening rather than diving straight in. 'Ah,' he said. 'No surprise there. Owns the company, does he? Or is he somebody else's bitch?'

'Oh no, he's in charge all right. Runs the whole shebang. And he's a hard-hearted motherfucker.'

'Sounds like my boss.'

'Oh? What do you do?' Rex was uncomfortable talking about himself.

'Oh, me? I'm a prospector, I suppose. I scrabble around in the dirt and I see if I can come up with a nugget. But my boss has very high standards when it comes to what sort of nuggets I come up with. There's a lot of fool's gold out there.'

'Sounds tough.'

'You have no idea. But never mind about my arsehole of a boss. You're the one that's been driven to chuck it in, so it must be serious. I'll let you tell me about it if you buy me a beer.'

'Sounds like a fair exchange,' said Rex, warming to the bloke. His interest seemed authentic. 'But only if you let me throw in another shot. That last one went down a bloody treat.'

'Done.'

They shared another shot and clinked their new beers together, and Rex got started on his story. At first, he tried to be circumspect about it, speaking in general terms about how his boss was a prick to his staff, used people to get what he wanted and was prone to throwing massive tantrums when things didn't go his way. Butch appeared not to be impressed.

'Sounds like every boss I ever had,' he said. 'Are you sure it's worth going on the dole for?'

'You don't understand; this guy's a megalomaniac. A

psychopath,' said Rex. 'And he did something I can't forgive to a friend of mine.'

'Ah. Now we're getting to it. I take it this friend works with you?'

'Well, kind of. Back in Perth.'

'Oh, it's a national company?'

'International. Only, not so much a company as an organisation. Well, a church.'

Butch's eyes widened and his nostrils flared, but he tried to look confused. 'A church? My friend, I think we definitely need another shot.'

And so it went for an hour and a half, then two, then three. Bit by bit, Rex gave up his whole story: who his boss was, what the organisation was ('I think I've heard of it,' said Butch with counterfeit uncertainty), and the murky business with Chloe. Butch weighed every answer and question with great care, and managed to weasel out every detail and nuance of Rex's months with the church and his weeks on tour with Casper, including the depth of his feelings for Chloe. He was suitably dismayed when Rex described the terrible scene with Skye, and he didn't have to pretend to be appalled when he heard about Tilly's treatment at Casper's hands.

As afternoon shifted into evening and Rex took on unaccustomed volumes of alcohol, he opened up more and more. He couldn't go back, he said. He'd kill Casper. Or at least make him a lot less pretty. So now he had nowhere to go, and he didn't know what to do. Worst of all, he was starting to think about what he'd given up.

'What do you mean?' Butch could scent a whole new line of enquiry.

'It's a secret,' said Rex, suddenly wary.

'Like I'm going to tell anyone,' replied Butch. 'Look at me. I doubt if I'll remember your name in the morning.'

'True. And you have been good to me,' said Rex. The ongoing purchase of shots had some time ago ceased to be a round and become the serial application of single shots to him alone, while Butch sat playing with his phone.

'Tell you what,' said Butch, looking around them with a conspiratorial air. 'Why don't we go back to my place for a feed, and you can tell me there? That way, there's no chance of prying ears listening in. The walls have ears in this joint.'

Frankly drunk by this time, but also hungry and ready to get off the stool he'd occupied for too long, Rex agreed. He wasn't certain this uninviting little fellow wouldn't try to come on to him, but he was sure that even in his current befuddled state he could beat him off. He started to giggle then, because to beat him off might just have been exactly what his new friend wanted.

'What's up?' asked Butch.

'Oh, nothing,' said Rex with a goofy grin. 'Let's do it. I'm so hungry I could take a bite out of a manhole cover and call it a pizza.'

'Hopefully it won't come to that,' said Butch.

Stepping on solid ground for the first time in several hours, Rex found out just how wobbly he was on his feet. Butch was at his elbow to lend a steadying hand, even though he was a trifle wonky himself. He seemed like such a nice bloke.

Winding their way back to Butch's digs only took five minutes. He was put up in a wretched low-rent hotel not far from the Cross: a temporary residence, he explained to Rex. They entered the compact suite, and Rex saw a kitchenette incompatible with cooking anything other than a piece of toast, a dining and living area strewn with paper and garbage, and an unmade bed over by a window looking at the brick wall next door. Moving ahead of his quarry, the host swept away piles of detritus and made a space for Rex on the grimy old couch, where he sat heavily. Butch put as many of the dozen cans of beer he'd bought as he could fit into the fridge, and brought a couple over to the living area. Before seating himself on a dining-table chair, he turned it around so he could watch and talk to his guest.

Once they had settled and a pizza was on the way, Butch broached the subject left hanging in the pub as subtly as he could. He scratched his head and put on a puzzled expression, cocked his head for a while as though thinking, and then spoke. He sounded uncertain, like he was trying to get his muddled mind back together.

'So, you say that by walking away from the church – which I must say would be the smart thing to do, because it sounds like your boss, this Casper guy, is a con artist – you'd be giving up something. What do you mean?'

Having taken a few moments of fresh air on the short walk, and feeling a fraction less inebriated, Rex was alarmed. Had he really given that much away? Should he try and be a little more guarded? Now he was wary. Not exactly alert, and certainly not up to the task of employing fine motor skills or complex reasoning, but a touch less malleable.

'I can't say,' he said.

'Why not?'

'It's church secrets.'

'So?'

'I gave my word.'

'You gave your word to that wanker? You've already told

me he's a psychopathic bully, so what's a promise to him worth? Come to that, what's his word worth?'

'Nah, I couldn't tell you. It's important.'

'Listen, if you tell me, I might just be able to help you find a way of getting back at your boss. Wouldn't you like that?'

'Well, yeah, but...' Rex was an honourable man, and he'd sworn an oath. On the other hand, Butch was right – Casper was the kind of bloke that would betray a vow at the slightest invitation. 'It might bring down the whole church.'

This was like finding a juicy pocket of marrow right in the last bit of bone to be chewed on – especially delicious because it was unexpected.

'Oh,' said Butch with exaggerated drama. 'In that case, better not to tell me. I mean, it's essential that your mate Casper gets to keep accumulating thousands of followers and squirreling away millions of dollars, and mistreating people, including your friends, whenever he feels like it. Am I right?'

'But you have to be high up in the church to know this stuff.' Rex was almost pleading, but he was also wavering. Butch could scent his desire to spill his guts.

'Look, why don't you just tell me what it is you'll be missing out on, and leave out the sensitive bits?'

Rex was torn. He wanted so much to tell this solicitous stranger, who'd been nothing but supportive all day, the whole story. But he wondered what Chloe might say if he did, and Coco and Yuki and Paris and the rest. Fuck Casper; he could go and fuck himself. But the others would be disappointed. And yet, if he didn't discuss it, and maybe get this very reasonable man's opinion on whether or not it might be true, he might even end up going back to Casper with his tail between his legs because he was terrified of missing out. Better to get the advice of a friend, and Butch had been very much that since they'd met.

'Well, you'll have to promise not to tell anyone,' he said.

Butch nodded eagerly and adjusted his phone so it sat midway between them. 'Wouldn't dream of it, mate,' he said with a wink.

'If I walk away from Felinism, I'll be giving up my chance to become the greatest builder in the galaxy,' he began. And from there he proceeded to relate the theory of Level Three Felinism in crude but accurate terms. He made a hash of a couple of the names, but covered most of the important points. Butch asked pertinent questions, did not have to simulate astonishment at the prophesied end of the Great Experiment, and got up a couple of times to refresh Rex's drink. The tale finished with Rex again expressing his regret that he could have been the builder to the stars, as it were, but hated Casper so much that he was willing to give it all up.

'It's all bullshit,' said Butch when Rex signified that he had completed his exposition by picking up the fresh beer in front of him and leaning back on the couch. 'And you know it.'

'Eh?' Rex hadn't quite expected that reaction.

'Come on, mate. You honestly believe that cats can talk to us with their minds? That they can order us about and get us to build things at their request? Why aren't all cats eating fillet steak and living in castles? My neighbour down in Melbourne has four of the scabbiest mongrels you ever saw, and they have to scavenge for scraps and they've all got the mange. Why don't they order her to lift her game?'

Rex explained that cats had, over the millennia, gone soft and lost many of their powers, while we humans had managed, through the unforeseen growth in our intelligence, to upset the balance of power and upend the hierarchy.

'Utter fucking crap,' was Butch's considered response. So Rex related what Casper had said to him.

'Almost everything that's created to serve, ends up being the master,' he said. He furnished the same examples – money, the press (which made Butch give a knowing laugh), cars, government and so on.

After ruminating on that for a little while, Butch cocked his head sideways and said, 'Well, he might be onto something there. But that spaceship stuff? The fairy tale about whizzing off to planet Meon to meet Bastet or whatever you call it? What a pile of bollocks.'

Rex winced but didn't say anything. He'd spent so long talking himself into believing Casper's dogma that it was hard to hear it described that way. It shocked him to realise that he was a true believer, but he also knew in his heart that Butch was right. It was all a beautiful lie. And now he was outside Felinism, he had to get back to believing in what was real. That would be easier said than done.

Butch helped, though. As they munched on pizza and ever more slowly drank beer, he gave voice to the practical objections any reasonable person might make to the fantastic invention of Felinism. He was more practised in the voluminous intake of alcohol than Rex, and had judiciously paced himself when Rex had consumed at a furious rate, so he was more lucid. Rex, for his part, took these objections at face value, and with each rebuttal of Casper's wafer-thin arguments, he felt better. He dropped off to sleep while Butch was holding forth on the actual evolution of cats and the domestication of *Felis lybica*.

36. Dogs are their own worst enemies

Nobody does sad and sorry like a dog. They're forever tucking their tails in under their arses, opening their big eyes wide with apology and begging forgiveness. And that's because they're stupid, blundering, reckless animals that break things first and think about it later. Dogs don't even need cats to be their foes, because they're their own worst enemies. Be like a cat.

Casper

Waking up on the short, lumpy couch in Butch's flat, Rex was dry, disoriented and queasy. He felt like he'd been tongue kissing a sand dragon, and he wondered how the drummer from Metallica could be doing the drum solo from *St. Anger* inside his head. He rolled over and fell straight off the couch, landing on an elbow and a hip, and even his low groan hurt his head.

'Fuck,' he said.

After a while, lying on the floor wasn't getting any more comfortable, and the pain in his scone wasn't getting any worse, so he sat up. It took a moment to figure out where he was and what he was doing there, but it all came flooding back when he stood up and looked at the apartment – if fragments from a bad dream, falling in disjointed dribs and drabs into his consciousness, could constitute a flood. There was a note on the table – *Stay as long as you like. Probably a good idea if you keep a low profile for a day or two. B.*

Keeping a low profile appealed to him, but he couldn't understand why Butch would think it appropriate too. No matter; he wasn't capable of going too far at the moment. He switched on the television and made himself a strong instant coffee in the meagre kitchenette. For the rest of the morning, he dozed and wallowed in the dross on the TV screen, listless and blank.

In the early afternoon, just as Rex was getting hungry, Butch turned up with a couple of Subway sandwiches and a welcome fizzy drink. The little bastard was distressingly cheerful and even healthy, which made Rex feel inadequate as well as nauseous.

'You know, I reckon I've figured it out,' said Butch between mouthfuls. 'Remember the opening of the Cat Life Centre over in Perth? I saw the way you looked at the manager lady, and the way you looked at Casper after that. I'm guessing she's Chloe?'

The alcohol-soaked blood in Rex's veins ran cold. Like, liquid nitrogen cold. What did Butch mean by that? He was there? How was that possible?

Sometimes trust is eroded, the way Rex's trust in Casper had been worn away by the constant drip, drip, drip of puerile acts, impatience, tantrums, spite and tyranny. And sometimes, trust collapses like a bamboo scaffold tied with raffia. Like a multi-storey building that's had its supporting columns removed explosively, all at once. This was one of those times.

As the entire edifice of his trust crashed down

around him, Rex knew he'd been set up. He cursed him-self for his gullibility and his willingness to see the best in people. Then the ramifications of placing his trust in this sneaky, underhanded prick came sheeting home to him. The words on the note made sense. He knew he was fucked, he just didn't know how.

'What have you done?' he asked, his voice hoarse and his head throbbing.

'I've done you a favour, mate,' said Butch. 'I've finally fixed that motherfucker's wagon. Laid out the foul truth of his cult for all to see – from preying on sexy young girls to the violent repression of his followers, to that whole cock and bull story about cats coming from outer space to make humans into their slaves. It's actually a very entertaining read. And it'll be all over the paper tomorrow. You're gonna be famous, mate.' He grinned and took a bite of his sub.

Dropping his head into his hands, smearing Thousand Island sauce on his temple, Rex discharged a squeaky 'fuck' and sank into despair. What had he done? He cradled his head like that for a good long time while Butch chewed on his Subway and swigged his Coke, unable to hold onto any thought that wasn't a four-letter expletive. But then it struck him: if he was going to have any chance of getting his stuff out of the pool house, he'd better do it before the shit hit the fan. Other -wise he'd never get near the Cat House, or any of the team.

He dialled Sebastian, who answered with a questioning, 'Hello?'

'Hey, Sebastian,' he said, trying to sound sunny. 'How are you doing?'

'Fine.' The answer was flat, and that alone told him that Sebastian, and by extension everyone else, was across the situation. They all knew that Chloe was 'gone,' and that Rex had walked off the reservation, so it was likely he would soon be *persona non grata*, if he wasn't already. Sebastian probably wouldn't be sure if he should be talking to a candidate for exile, but he was a kind, sensitive bloke, and Rex knew he could rely on him for help.

'Listen, I don't know what you've been told, mate, but I won't be coming back. I have to quit. And I can't get into the house to get my stuff. Could you maybe pack it up and get it to me?'

Sebastian sighed. It sounded like a big imposition. He wasn't sure what Rex's transgression had been or how Casper would react if he got wind of his helping him. But he liked Rex, and he was always ready to help a person in need. 'Well…'

'Please, mate, I'm desperate. I'm only down in the Cross, and there's not much stuff there – just a few clothes, my computer and charger and that sort of stuff. It won't take you half an hour.'

'Hmmm, I don't know. It could get me in trouble.'

'Oh, it won't, I promise. Casper won't even be thinking about that stuff, I guarantee it.'

'Okay, I'll do it now; there's not much going on and Casper and Paris are over in Bondi. Where?'

They set up a meeting in the bar at the Empire in twenty minutes, and Sebastian hung up. In the rush, Rex had forgotten what had led to this and he was actually happy for a millisecond after hanging up. Then he remembered, and his spirits plummeted. 'I'm a dead man,' he said.

37. Cats are aliens and we are their slaves

Casper White's cat cult is built on charisma, fantasy, oppression and money. Founded on brazen exploitation of the public's love for all things feline on the internet and backed by a bizarre theory of the alien origins of cats, White has created a massive money-making machine that directs millions straight into his bottomless back pocket. Sham is too kind a word for the Cat Man.

Butch McNab

Sebastian turned up on time, dropping off the bags that Rex hadn't unpacked properly since they'd moved into the house – he was used to being on the road. The transaction was completed without any ado; Sebastian was nervous, because although he didn't know the details, he was aware that Rex's name was now mud for the team, so he extricated himself as soon as he could.

Butch, who'd accompanied Rex to the bar, suggested they have a hair of the dog. Believing he couldn't feel any worse than he already did, Rex agreed and they had a few quiet beers. Butch explained that he hadn't named Rex in his article, so he should be safe, but Rex was unconvinced. Casper would know precisely where the information came from, and he would be livid. It wasn't beyond the realms of gruesome possibility that he would hunt him down and kill him for betraying the church. He'd promised as much at their meeting back in Perth.

The sun was down but it wasn't too late when they walked back to Butch's place and ordered a delivery from a local restaurant. The meal and the evening were mostly silent, each bent on his own thoughts, and each aware that the other's mood was the polar opposite of his own. Butch was excited because his reputation as a cult-buster was about to be raised to the skies; Rex was dejected and fretting about his future – if he had one at all.

Would Chloe ever talk to him? Would he go down in history as the man who'd brought down the Church of Felinism? What would happen to him if the cats should come back? He had two chances that they'd forgive him and take him on-board: slim and none.

No, no, no, he said to himself. The whole thing was a lie. There's no spaceship cats, no future on Meon, no intergalactic building program. He really had to move on, forget that he was ever part of that madness, go home and get back to good, honest labour. Chloe would probably never speak to him again, and in a year or two, or ten, or twenty, he would be over her too. He might one day meet a nice, simple girl who would care for him not because he was a dog or a cat, but because of the kind of man he was.

Later, he booked himself on a flight back to Perth for the next day. It would be good to go back to his homely home town, disappear into the suburbs and forget all this bullshit. He went to sleep still fearful about the fallout from Butch's article, but there was nothing he could do about it. The toothpaste wasn't going back into the tube any time soon. On Butch's advice, he turned off his phone.

Waking early, he found that Butch had managed again to get out without disturbing him, and hoped he was getting coffee. Rex's dreams had been torrid, filled with pursuit and danger, and enemies that lurked on every corner. It was cold in the tiny apartment, but he'd woken up a couple of times saturated in sweat and doused in fear. It wasn't restful in the least, and when he finally awoke for good, he didn't feel a whole lot better than he had the previous day. The booze nausea had been replaced by a stress knot in his guts and a tension headache caused by grinding teeth and the incessant flow of disturbing scenarios through his mind.

He watched the morning newstainment, which carried no mention of Casper or Butch. Yet. He was trying not to focus on what was coming when Butch bust open the door with his customary inelegance, bearing the treasured caffeine and a stack of *Sydney Morning Heralds* so tall it obscured his whole round head. He handed one to Rex with a coffee.

The front-page headline and main stories revolved around the standard issues of the day – impending war, recriminations over the last war, corrupt politicians pleading for clemency and forgiveness, improbable promises from politicians not yet revealed as corrupt. But at the top of the page was the item he'd dreaded to see – a square promo for a feature story to be found on pages four and five, with a photo of Casper holding a cat. The headline to that promo was, *Cats are aliens and we are their slaves.*

Ignoring the hoots of laughter from Butch at the look on his face, and feeling quite sick once again, Rex opened the paper to the second spread and cringed. The promo headline was repeated, spread in huge type across both pages, and there were a number of photographs, including a very large, clear one of Rex himself walking ahead of Casper in his security get-up, looking stern and powerful, and, he thought, kind of cool. But looking cool wouldn't save him now. Though Butch had assured him that his role in the story had been protected, the picture said it all. Everyone in the world would know exactly who the anonymous source was. *Fuck.*

The story was thorough, he had to give Butch that. Every dirty little detail of Casper's bad behaviour towards Tilly and Skye – and Chloe, goddammit – with the victims thankfully unnamed, along with lots of stuff about the financial irregularities repeated from the previous exposé, all put together very well in Butch's belligerent, cynical tone. The centre-piece was a ferociously mocking description of the upper levels of Casper's teachings about the prehistoric arrival of cats. Butch's bitterest scepticism was reserved for the idea that the cats would some day return to take Casper and his followers off to Meon for a life of voluntary slavery. Butch wondered whether it would be more just if the alien cats that took Casper and his cat people back to their mythical home world treated them the way earth cats treat the local fauna – as playthings for their diabolical blood sport.

Just reading the story gave Rex the heebie-jeebies, and in a real sense he began to fear for his life. He couldn't wait to get on that plane and back to Perth and disappear. But before Butch would let him sneak off to the airport, he made him turn his phone on and play the messages out loud. As expected, there were many, mostly from Paris, with several also from Coco and Yuki, at first asking him to call, and later expressing sorrow, anger and disgust at what he had done. There were also a couple of voice messages from Casper. The timbre of these was the same, and they had obviously all been delivered after the story had broken.

'You traitorous little bitch,' the Cat Man had ranted in the first. 'I'm going to cut off your balls, stuff 'em down your throat and pull 'em out through your arse. How fucking dare you do this to me, you pathetic pile of dog shit? I made you! And this is how you repay me? You and that fucking slut girlfriend of yours had better never show your faces ever again, or they will be cut off and mailed to your parents...' And so on – the next three were also in a similarly violent vein. Rex was horrified, but Butch grinned and patted him on the back. 'That's what you wanted, mate,' he said. 'Insurance. That moron has just threatened your life. You let him know that if anything untoward happens, or even looks like happening, this goes to the cops first, and the newspapers second. And you do it through a lawyer, just to be sure.' Butch chortled again. 'You've got him!'

Uncertain but affecting to be mollified, Rex nodded and smiled weakly.

'Don't for Christ's sake lose those messages,' said Butch.

Rex hit the play button again, for the final message. This one was from Chloe. Unbelievably, she was giggling.

'Oh, Rexy,' she tittered. 'What have you done? Did you do that for me? You are so sweet, although really you shouldn't have. But I'm glad you did. That bastard deserves everything he gets. Call me soon, mwah.'

He packed up his gear and ordered an Uber for the airport with a smile on his face.

38. Cats have nine lives

Cats can be more daring, take more risks and fewer prisoners, and tempt fate more than anyone else, because every one of their nine lives is charmed. Cats are tougher, smarter, more resilient and luckier than any creature alive, and if you want to share in their fortune, be more like them.

Casper

A few hours later, Rex was up in the air, and Casper had finally started to calm down. To say he was furious would do a grave disservice to fury. He was in an eye-popping, jugular-distending, stroke-inducing hysteria that set world records for blood pressure, spittle projection, face redness and profanity hurling. Expensive items were smashed, gouged, twisted, torn, battered, broken, cursed, crushed, flogged and sworn at in streams of vulgarity that made no sense and had no beginning or end. It was an epic dummy spit beyond any that even Paris had ever witnessed, and that no one in the Cat House ever wanted to see or hear again.

But even a hysterical frenzy of scabrous bestiality like

that peters out sooner or later, and the Cat Man's marathon rant came to an end when he at last ran out of invective and energy. To finish it off in true ignominy, he lay down and cried like a baby and whined like a teenager at the injustice and cruelty of it all. Why would anyone do anything like that to him, when he had only been a ray of sweetness and light that illuminated lives and created heightened consciousness wherever he went? At last he dropped off to sleep, and Paris closed the door on his shattered room with a prayer of thanks. Sometimes he was a handful.

With Casper sleeping off his conniption, Paris could settle down and deal with the situation. She crafted a press release in which she refuted the article with vigorous non-denials, suggesting that McNab had obtained his twisted, inaccurate and in places fanciful information from a drunk at a bar, at best an unreliable source and at worst an outright liar (she didn't specify which). She wrote that Casper had already, in a high-rating and well-received 60 Minutes appearance, addressed the nonsense about little green men (again, not a denial, but a well-placed deflection), rejected the 'unfounded gossip about mistreated church members,' and challenged McNab to find just one who would publicly admit to having suffered such abuse. She was certain that none of the current members of the church would contemplate such a betrayal, and she knew very well that the extremely generous settlement which she had negotiated, and which contained a rigorous non-disclosure agreement, meant Tilly would never raise her pretty head above the parapet.

She concluded by scoffing at 'hearsay' about money laundering, embezzlement and tax issues in a different country to that in which the slander was published, pointing out that there was no suggestion at all that Casper or the church had committed any financial irregularities in Australia.

'It's too easy to level unanswerable accusations about what might have gone on in a country half a world away,' she wrote. 'It speaks of sloppy journalism, blind malice, and seeking personal advancement at the expense of a popular public figure whose only crime is to be above the likes of any "journalist" who would pen such nonsense.' A postscript to the release offered to sue any media outlet that repeated unsubstantiated allegations, and suggested that Butch McNab and the paper he wrote for would soon find themselves on the receiving end of a punishing libel suit.

It was a masterclass in spin, truth-dodging and fact-bending, and it got every bit as much airplay as Butch's accusations. Once again, the members of the church sprang to Casper's defence, threatened boycotts and protests of participating media, and mocked and derided Butch McNab without mercy. Moneyed members threatened their own lengthy lawsuits, and the withdrawal of investment funds from and costly disruptions to the business of any medium that pursued the story, including the revocation of advertising contracts.

The result of all of this was that the story was put to rest soon after it had been born, and the editor of the Sydney Morning Herald was heard to declare that Butch McNab could forget about ever darkening his door again.

By the time Rex landed in Perth, the story was already dying, and though it went through a few throes before finally carking it for good, it was clear to all that it was terminal. Casper had won again.

39. Every dog has his day

Cats — and cat people like us — can have bad days; we are not immune to the vagaries of life. And even the mangiest, dumbest dog will occasionally catch a break. That's life. Don't begrudge the dog when he has his day — let him wag his tail and think that everything will be okay. We all know that somehow, some day soon, a cat will make his life hell again.

Casper

It was one of those wet winter days when Perth people stop saying, 'It's good for the farmers,' and say, 'For fuck's sake, when will this rain stop?' It had been bucketing down for days on end and everything was soaked. When the wind wasn't howling from the northwest, it was freezing from the south-west. Great puddles that resembled small lakes had formed on roads built with drainage more suited to the odd shower than ongoing downpours, and drivers everywhere were getting snarly, snarky and even more offensive than usual.

In the back of the Uber heading to his place, Rex reflected on the last five months. It was hard to believe that Chloe had only arrived home from America in February, and harder still to credit that just two months had passed since he'd set off with Casper and the girls on their tour.

So much had happened – so much water down the drain of a life suited for the odd shower rather than the deluge of events, emotions and surprises that had inundated him ever since he'd met Casper.

It was a lonely homecoming. He wasn't returning in glory but slinking in through the back door. He couldn't wait to curl up on his rug and chew its corners in the dark, ruminating on an uncertain future whose only hope was that it wouldn't be as bad as the recent past. He'd go back to work in a week or so, maybe, but in the meantime, he'd burrow in and pretend he was a bear, hibernating until things got less frosty. He debated whether or not to throw away his phone, because it was unlikely to bring good news or happy invitations any time soon. But as always, there was one thing stopping him from doing that.

In spite of it all, he could never walk away from Chloe. Christ alone knew what she was thinking, let alone what she would do, but he would be true until the end, or at least until he met that mythical girl who could take his mind off her. As always, he vacillated between aching with love and concern for Chloe, and despair at the way she had treated him. And as always, love won.

He knew that all she had to do was click her fingers and he would come running, do her bidding without question and lap up even her merest attentions like they were ambrosia. All she had to do was call. But the phone remained silent, day and night. That was a mixed blessing, because it meant that he wasn't at the top of Casper's hit list right then, but he also wasn't on Chloe's radar.

As the days trickled into nights and still there was no word from Casper, Paris or the Church of Felinism, Rex became convinced that Casper's way of dealing with the situation had been to banish it from his mind and to order everyone else to do the same. Rex and Chloe would join countless others in having been excommunicated from the church and expunged from memory. That was a relief.

Four days of pretending that the outside world didn't exist was enough. At heart, Rex was a gregarious creature, and more than that he was a doer. Wasting away inside was not his style. The appalling weather had given way to those clear, bright, shiny days between storm events that can make Perth a magical place to enjoy a winter's day, and he spent half an hour getting his car started before heading out to join his work crew on-site towards the end of the fourth day. They'd ploughed on without him for the last few months, but he was back to take the helm. He thanked his lucky stars that he hadn't rented out his house or sold his business when he'd gone off on his ridiculous adventure. He wondered where his beautiful new four-wheel drive was right then, but wouldn't have been surprised if Casper had torched it just to see it burn.

In any case, his team was pleased to see him and would be happy to have him back on-site the next day, which was encouraging. He joined the crew at the pub for a quick post-work beer and caught up on their antics, while they were kind (or apathetic) enough not to mention his own escapades. It was beginning to feel like it had never happened.

As he drove into his driveway that night, his phone pinged. He assumed it was his foreman updating him on their plans for the next day. He forgot about it while he hauled his takeaway inside, and it was only half an hour later, after he'd licked the grease off his fingers, that he thought to look at the message.

Three words: 'Where are you?' From Chloe. He sent a message saying, 'At home,' and waited for the call. He assumed she would rake him over the coals for his betrayal of Casper and the church. He hadn't forgotten that message from her before he'd left Sydney, but that, he'd decided, was probably an aberration. He expected that she would have reconciled with Casper and was about to deliver some kind of warning or threat. But the phone didn't ring. Weird.

Half an hour later, there was a sharp rap at the front door. Surely not? He almost broke his legs tripping over the furniture and his own feet to get to the door, and when he'd flung it open, sure enough there she stood. Glowing. Utterly, outrageously beautiful and flawlessly dressed as always – the kind of picture he had always hoped he would be able to recall in years to come when he thought of her with fond sadness. That petite baby bump, though, as sweet and full of promise as it was, had never been a part of his fantasy for this moment.

Without warning, Chloe threw herself into his arms and wrapped her own around his neck. 'Oh, Rex,' she said in a voice laden with emotion. 'I've been such an idiot.'

The scent of her was intoxicating, and the feel of her was luxuriant. He was instantly in heaven, even if a tiny piece of him was on guard for the next bit. The sentence that would come with the inevitable, 'but…'

'Can I come in?' she asked as she disentangled herself and drew away.

'Of course.' He wished he'd cleaned up a bit better; the house was kind of a hovel after almost a week of ascetic withdrawal.

She sat on the couch, having shoved aside a couple of

unsavoury items like wrappers and a blanket that looked and smelled rather rank, and motioned for him to sit beside her.

'You've always been so good to me, Rex,' she began. 'I've been a bitch; I know I have. But the way you did what you did to Casper – that was for me, right?'

It had been the last straw, but she didn't need to know that. In fact, even without all that other stuff, he probably would have done it for her anyway. He nodded.

'You're such a wonderful friend, and a beautiful man, Rex.'

He kept waiting for the 'but…'

'And I haven't just been a bitch, I've been a fool. Do you know, it was only when you were away that I realised just how much you mean to me. I know, I know. Whenever I called, I talked about Casper, but I know now that that was just my way of getting around the fact that it was you I wanted to talk to. It's taken me ages to admit that to myself. But it's true.' She stared into his eyes, and he felt like he was a frog in a biology class and the teacher had just cut him open and laid his heart on the table for all to see.

'But…' She hesitated. Here it came: part two. The dismissal. Why would she come here just to rip his soul out again?

'But I've been such a shit to you, I don't know how you're going to take this.'

He steeled himself for the next part.

'I went to the doctor today, Rex, and it turns out I was wrong. I thought I was ten weeks along, but I'm closer to twelve.'

'Huh?'

'The baby.' She smiled, a frank, happy, relieved and hopeful smile. 'It's not Casper's at all. It's yours. Will you have us?'

THE CAT MAN

\